GW00401267

Dance with Life

Dance with Life

J.M. Hurley

Published by Katy Press

Katy Press
2 Barrack Street, Bantry,
Co Cork, Ireland

www.katy-press.com

First Edition 2004

Copyright © J.M. Hurley 2004

J.M. Hurley asserts the moral right and her rights under the
Copyright, Designs and Patents Act, 1988 to be identified
as the author of this work

A catalogue record for this book is available from
the British Library

ISBN 0-9547811-0-4

All rights reserved.
No part of this publication may be reproduced, stored in a
retrieval system, or transmitted, resold, hired out or otherwise
circulated in any form or by any means, electronic, mechanical,
photocopying, recording or otherwise,
without the prior permission of the publishers.

Printed and bound in Great Britain by Cox & Wyman
Reading, Berkshire.

For all who thirst for more...

For M - Thank you for teaching me this dance

For my parents who supported me even when it baffled them!

For all teachers everywhere...

Author s Note

This book is written as a fictionalised story, but is based on real experience and real feeling. From Act I onwards the story is situated in the imagination and heart of the main character, Mira. Her day to day life continues on as normal, but I leave out almost all reference to her daily life and concern myself only with what she is learning, experiencing and feeling as she travels on the road of her own heart. I do this because from my own experience the process of inner learning very often continues in a symbolic and synchronous way, in tandem with the flow of day to day life.

Prologue

'Do you know what it means to be alive?' he asks.

'Do you understand that life is only a moment, just one moment after another?

Do you understand that?

There is no going back, no skipping ahead, just the moment called now, just the feeling that you carry within you.

Do you realise how much time is lost by spending all the yesterdays dreaming of tomorrows?

All the 'should haves' and 'could haves' are meaningless.

Tragedy is when you realise this too late.

Tragedy is when the first experience and understanding of this reality comes with the last breath.'

She looks at him and sees the universe dance in his eyes. Who is he? She's not sure, but the clarity in his gaze melts all doubt from her heart. In meeting his gaze she can feel the feeling of which he speaks. It is the most profound. It is a homecoming. She never wants to leave. He looks away and she is cut adrift. He smiles.

'If you want this feeling,' he continues, 'if you want

this kind of love, I can help you find it. It is within you. You cannot meet me at the crossroads. You must make a commitment to your own journey. No one else can do this for you. But just take one step towards me and the universe itself will bend to meet you.'

O

She stood at the crossroads a long, long time. Moons passed, clouds rolled by, suns rose and yet there she stood. Waiting. What was she waiting for? Perhaps a signpost to appear, a marker that would shout a direction to her. In her heart there was silence.

Mira had thought about what he had said, and about how it had made her feel, over and over again. She hadn't been trekking in India. She hadn't been on a vision quest in the South American rainforests. She was an advertising executive, working in a city, living with a partner that she loved. She had great friends, a loving family. Life was mostly good. It wasn't perfect, but it was normal. There were things she'd change if she could. Her job was tough, her apartment was the size of a shoe-box and the frantic pace of city life got her down sometimes, but for the most part she was happy. She hadn't sought this out. She didn't think she had been looking for something more. But his words, heard back then in the dry surrounds of a conference hall, had touched a part of her of which she hadn't been aware. They had awakened a longing, a thirst for more, a thirst to explore. She had seen much of the world. She knew a lot about living, but did she really know what it meant to be alive? When she found that she couldn't answer this question it had stopped her in her tracks. And could he, this small Buddha-shaped man with his business suit and his laughing eyes, really take her to an answer? She had returned, week after week, to listen to him some more and every time the feeling returned, the sense that she was where she was supposed to be, the feeling that she was home. And, each time, her longing grew, her longing to feel that sense of home in her own heart. He had said that it only took one step to start the journey. Now she felt ready to begin. She knew this journey wouldn't be to a distant land, it would be a voyage to the world inside. The crossroads was in her own heart and now she stood there, waiting.

* * *

She closed her eyes. A warm breeze blew softly on her skin. She felt something flutter in the air. She opened her eyes. A butterfly was flapping merrily around her head. She put her hand out as if to try to touch it. The butterfly slowed and landed on her hand. Then it took off and whirled upwards in a giddy flurry of movement before coming back to rest again on her open palm. She looked at it. It was a very simple butterfly, just plain white with a little black face. It seemed to be laughing. She felt that she could almost hear its laughter tinkling up at her earnest expression. Then it was off again in another spiralling flourish, its tiny wings flapping earnestly against the currents of air. It went to the edge of a nearby path and just let itself drop down in the sudden fall of an air pocket. She smiled to herself, realising that choosing a direction didn't matter, she just had to make the decision to proceed. She followed the butterfly to the edge and looked down. She found herself standing on a little ledge, overhanging a winding path not far below. She gazed down at the path. The sky had turned a golden orange. The clouds rolled in from the sea; their salt smell mingling with the dusky musk of the damp heather that carpeted the rolling headland. The path was bathed in the mixed hues of the evening sky. It shimmered lilac and gold. It stretched far into the horizon.

She jumped.

She did not jump to destruction. She jumped to salvation. She landed with a soft thud on a bed of white heather.

The universe watched. Perched on a rock in the distance was another butterfly. This one was a rainbow

13

of colours. It sparkled and shone. The butterfly flapped its wings. From its iridescence, a poem of light emerged. The colours spread to the four corners of the world, merging with the seas and mists, becoming translucent, hiding their magic in the soft cloak of air.

The wings flapped again.

She felt a stirring in her soul. A sensation of a little voice trying to clear its throat. She sat quietly. In that one small jump everything had changed. She felt different. A longing coursed through her veins. What had been a curiosity, what had been a sensation to go on, the urge that had pushed her to jump, had now become a deafening roar. It had the bittersweet taste of longing, mingled with the certain knowledge that the longed for was now within her grasp.

The wings flapped again.

The world shifted, just a small degree in all directions, but the shift happened and he was there. She looked up and fell into his eyes.

'I've been waiting,' he said, smiling.

'What now?' she whispered.

He let her fall from his eyes and in their reflection she

saw worlds she had never even imagined.

'Now the dance begins,' he murmured.

She took a deep breath. She was nervous but not afraid. She didn't know where he would take her only that she wanted to go. He looked at her gently.

'This is not a journey with outcomes,' he said. 'The journey is the destination. I can accompany you on this journey but it is your journey and I cannot take your steps for you. You need to feel it in your own heart. Face it with clarity and with courage.'

He held out his hand. She reached up and took it.

Act I

He turned to her and, putting his hand to the side of his mouth, gently blew over the top of her head.

In a quiet unseen place a butterfly emerged from a chrysalis. Slowly, carefully, it began to unfold its tiny wings. The wings were a delicate silvery green. The butterfly flapped its wings.

The world shimmered. The sky dissolved. Then Mira felt she was the sky and was in its core. Stars swirled past. She saw them form, from birth to death and the space in between. She felt light, as if balancing on a leaf in the heart of existence. She saw that the universe was far from being a silent empty place. It was pulsing with life. It was a cyclical dance of light and energy. She saw that every breath she took contained elements of the dance. She saw that every breath was precious and that, in the spaces in between, there was a stillness; and yet, even that very stillness pulsed. Its pulse was love, a tremendous love that was wider than the universe, a love that contained an infinity of universes. Borders blurred. She felt that she was as much inside each breath as outside. She thought that she could as easily be in an atom of her own being as she could be an atom in the being of the universe. She was wrapped in the deep velvet blue of the dark sky.

She opened her eyes and saw the universe flow back into his eyes. She felt his gaze work like a physical force penetrating into the depths of her soul. It left everything stripped in its wake: pretensions, fears, dreams, ambitions, hopes, loves, hates; all were cast aside by the force of this feeling. She realised that she was really being seen for the first time in her life.

His gaze came to rest in a part of her of which she had been only dimly aware. It was the essence of her heart and it hummed with the simplest peace. It was home.

'How lightly we use the word home,' she thought. To feel that home was beyond anything she could have imagined. It was a solid place. It was brimming with love and acceptance. She felt the tears trickle from her eyes.

'I had no idea that I had this place within me,' she said.

He was thoughtful.

'For many this is the destination,' he said. 'But it is not the destination. It is the anchor. Fall in love with this feeling, it is the steady state. It is the place you must start out from at the beginning of every day and it is the place to which you must always return. Even in one day, even in one moment it is possible to forget where true home is. From here you can truly explore because the heart is the truest compass. I have opened you to the language of the heart. With practice you will become fluent.'

She was confused.

'But I just want to stay with this feeling now,' she exclaimed. 'Why would I want to go any where else?'

He shook his head.

'You have been introduced to you,' he said 'now get acquainted. Get to know you in all your aspects but always remember to come home. The knowledge of the self has its own momentum. It will take you where you need to go. You must take the next steps.'

'I don't understand,' she said. 'What am I to do?'

'Just trust,' he replied. 'I will be right behind you, though it may not always be apparent to you. We are joined now by a cord of love. If I see you stray too far I'll give a tug to remind you to return.'

He smiled gently and was gone. This time she was not adrift.

Act II

He beckoned to her. His eyes were still and calm. He held out his hand. She looked and saw that he was holding a key. His gaze became serious. She realised that he was contemplating his next action. Without saying a word he handed her the key. She accepted it.

'This is a gift,' he said. 'It is given with trust. Treasure it.'

Her heart felt full. She was beyond words. All that came was a simple 'Thank you.'

'Explore for a while, I'll see you later,' he said as he turned to leave.

Mira looked around her. She saw the door almost at once. A halo of light danced around its edges. She walked towards it. In the centre was a small keyhole. She put the key in. It was a perfect fit. She turned the key and heard the smooth click of the lock opening. The door creaked open a little and light poured out. It was dazzling. Pushing the door open, she walked through and found herself standing in a beautiful garden.

A golden butterfly swam into her vision. The butterfly flapped its wings. It began to transform. It grew and grew. It stretched upwards, folding its wings back into itself. Its wings became a gown of light and colour. Within the light a being formed. The being was female, with sea green eyes and hair that tumbled down in a tangle of golden waves. Light flowed from the centre of her forehead and from her palms. She stood with her hands outstretched, her head tilted to the sun. The sea swirled at her feet. All around her the wind crashed and howled, and yet the air seemed still. She turned to look at Mira and began to speak. Her voice had a power that resonated to the distant mountains.

'I am destiny,' the Being said. 'I move in the circle of light. I fear no one. I am the dark goddess and I am the queen of light. In me duality has no voice. All is one.'

She raised her right hand and thrust it to the sky. A streak of lightening flashed from her palm and crackled through the rolling clouds.

'I control the power and I am the power. I can create and destroy. I am protection.'

She raised her left hand and held it outward, her palm facing the ground. A ray of pink light flowed from her palm and fell on the closed bud of a flower. As the light gently enfolded the flower, Mira saw its petals begin to open and the beautiful flower almost seemed to reach upwards, its little head eagerly tilting towards the glowing light.

'I look soft as a sunbeam. I am as indestructible as the diamond. In me love is all.'

She looked at Mira and the light poured from her forehead filling Mira's mind. In an instant Mira saw glimpses of her life, events that had happened, what was happening now and events that were still to come.

'I am your learning. You cannot feel my light until you have understood my darkness. See through my eyes. Hear through my ears. Energy is a force, a fuel. I can give you anything you desire.'

Mira stood transfixed.

'Where did you come from?' she asked.

'I am in you,' the voice replied. 'I carry the secret blueprint of your existence. When I speak, your stomach stirs.'

She placed her hands on Mira's stomach and Mira felt a shudder, as if a current of electricity had passed through her.

'My connection point is there,' the voice continued, 'I am the guide, the gut feeling, the foreboding, the symmetry. Listen to me and you will not falter.'

She moved one hand to Mira's heart.

'He teaches the language of the heart and I teach the language of the gut. Once the course of the heart is set my role is to ensure that you do not stray. To stray will bring you pain, because it is necessary. In choosing to follow you choose to lead. Remember this.'

The light dissolved. The Being began to fade. Mira found herself alone once more, strangely agitated and utterly perplexed. Her mind became fuzzy from the sheer effort of trying to understand what she had just experienced. She felt like she was being pulled in two directions. A part of her wanted to float off and become as insubstantial as the air, while the other part felt so solid and heavy that it seemed to be rooted to the spot. She didn't quite know what to do with either. She felt in the middle, unable to understand either place very well and yet she was filled with the thirst to explore. She closed her eyes and the peace of home settled on her with the softness of a flower enfolding its petals against the cold of the night.

His voice floated through her heart.

'What did you learn?' he asked.

'I really don't know,' she replied.

He laughed heartily.

'Very good,' he exclaimed. 'To be able to say you don't know is always an honest starting point. What do you feel?'

'It's like there are two of me at the moment. I felt a power when she touched me, a sense that I could be her, that I could have all the answers, all the power but that there would be consequences if I didn't make the right choices. There was an aspect to her that really terrified me, yet she said she was in me. How could that be?'

'The inner voice can see in all directions,' he replied. 'To know yourself you must get to know your capacity in all directions. Good and bad are not qualities that exist outside. They are inside every human being. To be unaware of this would be to mislead yourself. Take time, let this settle. Look at what is around you; see things for what they are. Sometimes this will involve just seeing something exactly for what it is. Sometimes it will be to look beyond what is apparent. Listen to your gut feeling it is often a very good mouthpiece for the heart.'

The voice faded and she slept.

Act III

A butterfly flitted and hovered. Its wings were deep red with flecks of gold. It saw the garden and came to rest on a rose. It flapped its wings once, then sat quietly basking in the midday sun.

Mira opened her eyes and found that she was sitting under a willow tree. The garden was alive with life. The insects hummed and buzzed. Birds sang and squirrels darted to and fro. Sunlight sparkled on the water of a large pond in the centre of the garden. The pond itself was awash with water lilies. The smell of jasmine filled the air and mingled with the scent of roses and lavender. It was an intoxicating and heady mix.

'This place is so alive', she thought, 'that it's almost overpowering.'

A little boy ran towards her.

'Look!' the child exclaimed, 'I've got a kitten. Isn't he beautiful!'

She looked at the kitten and at the excited eyes of the child. The kitten blinked up, its tiny orange eyes squinting, in a silky black face, against the sunlight.

'What's his name?' she asked the boy.

'He's called Amber, because my Mommy says he's got amber eyes. Amber is another word for orange you see,' he explained helpfully.

'Where is your Mommy?' she asked.

'Over there with Daddy,' he replied pointing to a clearing in the hedge.

She walked over to take a look. The father was asleep and the mother was planting flowers in a bed of freshly dug earth. The mother smiled at her. She was heavily pregnant and stood up slowly. She was young and pretty, with dark skin and long black hair. She cuddled the boy affectionately.

'Let Amber go back to his mother now, he's ready for his supper. You can go and find your sister and play with her for a while,' she said to the child.

He placed the kitten near a silver Persian cat that purred and stretched lazily in the sun. The cat reached out a paw to direct Amber to a teat. Three other kittens were already sucking busily. She noticed that two kittens were silver and the other, like Amber, was a silky black. Sitting on a nearby stone, washing a carefully positioned paw, was a large black tomcat. He glanced over and in that glance the orange glint of his eyes sparkled with a nonplussed pride.

'Obviously daddy cat,' Mira remarked to the mother.

'Oh yeah, he's a character that one!' the mother laughed reaching out to tickle the tomcat's ear. 'It's all life here,' she added. 'We're all busy producing the next generation.'

She patted her stomach to emphasise. Still smiling she continued, 'I love to plant and to get my hands in the earth. Life is so intense at times that feeling the earth is the sure way to remember that we're all made up of the same stuff at the end of the day. And of course it's where we end up. Do you know that that frightens some people?'

She let some earth fall through her open fingers.

'Isn't it Eliot that said "I can show you fear in a handful of dust"?'

Mira nodded.

'Does it frighten you?' she asked the mother.

'No,' the mother replied. 'I can't control the seasons. I can only bend and flow to time and all the while tend to my garden, keeping it fresh and alive. It's continuous you know. If I even take a day's break the weeds are there, but I can only do so much. I'm part of it and when my winter comes I will accept it. Knowing that winter will come makes the other seasons more enjoyable though, don't you think?'

She looked thoughtfully at Mira.

'I hadn't thought of it like that,' Mira replied. 'But

yes, it's the contrast that makes it all so remarkable.'

The mother smiled and nodded in agreement. Mira looked around her, trying to imagine what the garden would look like during the various seasons of the year. Her reverie was interrupted by the low buzz of a bee. The bee landed on a flower and its little legs busily set to work on pollen collection.

'Honey for the bee', she thought, 'and beauty for me.'

As if reading her thoughts the mother murmured, 'the flower is useful and beautiful at the same time and all we have to do is to enjoy it.'

The mother was on her knees again, her concentration returning to her flowerbed.

Mira walked on. She saw the familiar figure approach. His eyes danced. 'Well what are you learning?' he asked.

'That nature is so beautiful and amazing,' she gushed. 'To my eyes it's just one beautiful picture, but I see that when you look at it from the viewpoint of the garden that it's a very busy workplace. Everything has its own function in this garden and it could all just look functional but it doesn't and that's the incredible part. It's all fragrant and beautiful as if it were there just to please my senses.'

'Good!' he said, 'you're looking with clear eyes. The

cycles of life flow in the garden. It is a teacher. Enjoy the fragrances here and now because they have their season and nothing can stop the natural cycles of life from progressing. Now, continue on', he said, winking at her as he strolled away.

Act IV

She walked for a while before returning to the mother and the sleeping father. The father stirred and opened his eyes. He looked at Mira and smiled at his wife.

'Ah you should have woken me up to tell me we had company!' he exclaimed. He sprang to his feet. He was tall and strong with a mane of ginger hair and deep blue eyes.

'You like gardens?' he asked her.

She nodded.

'Then you must see my vegetable garden.'

He led her off towards a high wall. There was a door in the wall and he led her through. Stretching out in front of her were rows of perfectly managed crops. Fruit trees lined the edge and a large walk-in cloche at the end was brimming with tomatoes, peppers and exotic fruits. A large vine dripping grapes covered one end of the cloche.

'Make my own wine from these,' he winked. 'A little of what you fancy I always say.'

He laughed heartily.

'I make wine from pumpkins and rhubarb too. We have great Tasting Parties at the end of the summer

– you must come! Anyway look here,' his hand swept towards the rows of vegetables, 'we're an eat all you see kind of family. Have to battle the pests though, and not all the crops are successful, but by planting enough diversity we never go hungry. If times get tough - and they often do,' he added ruefully, 'I can get work as a bricklayer.'

He patted the solid brick wall that surrounded the vegetable garden.

'Built all these walls myself,' he said proudly. 'Have to keep busy me! I like to be active, so when the weather's against the crops I get my tools and head to town.'

She looked at him in admiration.

'You're an amazing family,' she said softly. 'You inspire me to tackle my own sadly neglected garden!'

'Good, good,' he replied enthusiastically. 'A gardener in the making! Patience in all things, that's the true motto of a gardener. Can't force the seeds up, they have to do it in their own time.'

They walked along one of the little paved pathways that ran through the vegetable beds.

'As you can see it's very structured here. It has to be because it's our food supply. I don't allow the children or animals to play in here. They know the rules – no messing around in here or taking bites from the crops!

And definitely no interference in this section.'

He gestured to a long stretch of herb beds.

'This looks pretty, but it's what I call the hospital. Everything here has a medicinal use and some of these plants are dangerous if taken incorrectly. I sell these also in the town - healthy money eh!' he added with a laugh.

He nodded and smiled happily to himself as he looked proudly at his garden. Then he turned and led her back, animatedly pointing out this and that feature along the way. She returned with a happy heart to sit for a while longer under the willow tree, absorbing all the sights, sounds and smells of the garden and listening to the laughter of the children darting after their full-bellied kittens.

She saw a figure silhouetted in the evening sun. The figure drew nearer and she could see his smile.

'Are you still learning then?' he asked playfully.

'I think so,' she replied.

'And what are you learning?' he asked with a slow smile.

She looked at him a bit suspiciously. She wasn't sure whether he was being serious or whether he was just teasing her, but she decided to opt for serious.

'I'm learning that there is a need for order and for

rules also. My instinct is to let everything just flow free but I can see why some things have to be ordered and to be kept out of bounds until you have the skills to understand how to manage them.'

He smiled and nodded. 'Yes, every choice made in life comes with a set of consequences,' he said. 'Responsibility is part of life. There are certain needs that have to be met. You need money to live. If you have a family then they must be provided for. These are not burdens, nor are they obstacles. True responsibility is in accepting the choices made and in undertaking them with a joyful heart. Everything you need to do in life must be done with the same desire for perfection as you bring to your inner journey.'

'But surely not everything is enjoyable,' she questioned. 'There are times that you have to do things you really don't enjoy. Work isn't always fun. It can be really terrible!' she exclaimed.

'Then you are in the wrong job,' he replied flippantly. 'Of course life isn't always plain sailing, but that is very different to what I am talking about. I am talking about the consciousness you bring to your every task. The key is in really being clear about what you want to do in your life on every level, then setting on the path to achieve that. That is what taking responsibility means. Too many people sit on the fence complaining about what they don't want to do and where does that get you? Nowhere! Knowing what you don't want to do is a circular process; it begins in misery and complaint and ends right back in the same state. Fixing your sight on what you do want to do, and actively going about the process of achieving that, means that when you have to go though difficult patches they are bearable. And why? Precisely because you are very clear on why you are going through them and on where they are leading you. Do you understand this?'

'I understand,' she nodded.

'When the wrong choice has been made,' he continued, 'then it has to be faced head-on and corrected. The point is not to say 'I have made this choice and so now I have to suffer the consequences'. When suffering enters the equation it's just an excuse to avoid necessary change. Responsibility is about making change consciously and honestly. It is not about blame or finger-pointing, nor is it about causing others to suffer because you haven't taken the time to be clear.'

He smiled, then turned to leave. She watched his silhouette fade into the sunset and, still digesting what she was learning, began to drift off to sleep as the warm dusk settled across the sky.

Act V

The gentle tap on her shoulder woke her.

'How are you?' a voice asked.

It was him. She looked around but could see nothing; she was in total darkness.

'Where am I?' she asked sleepily.

'You're at the place of union,' he replied. 'This is where all the points meet.'

'I can't see anything,' she said.

'Any thing and no thing are the same,' he said. 'That is the resolution of duality. Your eyes may not be able to see but your heart can. What do you feel?'

'I feel peace and calm,' she answered. 'I don't feel any more than that. It's a sense that it has always been like this and will always be.'

'Look harder now. Is it really dark?' he urged.

She looked. The effort of looking strained her eyes and she closed them. As soon as she closed her eyes she could see light all around her. It wasn't like physical sunlight. It wasn't even as if she was actually seeing physical light, it was more of a sense of clear and limitless light flowing in all directions at once.

She opened her eyes and it was still dark but the

feeling of light remained.

'Though it appears to be dark and my logic tells me it's dark, I have a sense of profuse light,' she said, sounding confused.

'And because you feel this light do you really believe that it is still dark?' he asked.

'I can't,' she replied, 'because the sense of light is so strong it's impossible to believe that it's really dark. I mean it is dark, but not, if you know what I mean.'

He laughed.

'Yes I do know what you mean. Real experience and feeling comes from within. It shapes what is real. The inner light is the light of the heart. When that light shines, it overpowers all darkness. Now what you physically see is just an absence. If I remove this curtain then the sunlight will pour in, but it won't matter because the inner light is constant. It is always there. So dark outside, light outside doesn't matter, it is what is inside that counts. Light is a real thing. It overpowers darkness on every level. I can't remove another curtain and let darkness in to engulf the light. I can only create darkness by blocking out the light, but the light is always there, waiting for a chink through which it can pour. Even the smallest spark, the tiniest chink will let the light in. Never forget that. Even when it seems to be the darkest place, never forget that the light is there, waiting for the moment when you allow it to seep in.'

As she was thinking about what he was saying, he drew the curtain and light flooded the room.

'Now I can see you,' he laughed. 'But you can't see you, you can only see me!'

He laughed even harder.

'You can only see me too!' she quipped in reply.

'Yes!' he exclaimed, 'because we're in these amazing bodies with eyes that only see in one direction. But I just showed you that there is another way to see with a different part of your being.'

He paused.

'See this hand,' he continued, holding one hand up, 'imagine it's your physical self with all its hopes and dreams. It has a finite route. It is made of the elements and it will return to the elements. Now see this hand,' he said, holding the other up, 'imagine this is the place inside that you have just experienced. This has been, is, and always will be.'

He joined his hands, interweaving the fingers. He smiled.

'This is life. This is the merger of the finite and the infinite. Through the amazing feeling machine that is your finite self, your infinite nature can play in the symphony of life. With every breath the finite and the infinite meet. Their point of union is contained in that breath. It's as close as the two realms can ever get to one another. The point of being alive, of understanding the nature of this breath is to feel and to experience this gift of life.'

She reflected on what he was saying. Questions flooded her mind.

'Then why,' she asked, 'feel the inner feelings so strongly? Why have the wish to stay in that still place if the purpose is to enjoy a physical experience?'

'To learn and to balance,' he answered, 'It's a dance. Does an astronaut begin to put the space suit before everything else, or does he see it as a tool he can use to explore unknown lands? Do you weep and mourn each time you throw a nail clipping in the fire?'

She shook her head.

'The answer is 'no',' he continued, 'because you can see the real purpose and limitation of each. With life it's trickier. You can forget that the true nature is made up of two parts. You can lose perspective and begin to value one over the other. But both are necessary, and both need to live in harmony. When one gets out of step the other naturally stumbles. That is the nature of the dance; both parties have to be in step to keep the dance moving and fluid. You have seen that the heart is a beautiful place and that the world can be a beautiful place. But it's not always so easy. Remember that as your own dance continues. The true explorer is only an explorer when he knows where his home is and returns there regularly to replenish. Without that return, without that acknowledgement of home then he is simply lost.'

'I just can't imagine how anyone could forget to return,' she exclaimed.

'Ha!' he chortled. 'Be careful. There are many things that can give the illusion of that place. It only takes one moment of unconsciousness, one glance to the side to miss the turning and become lost. The wise person stops and asks for directions, the fool thinks that if he just keeps going then he'll eventually find his way back. And eventually he just might, but look at how much time is lost in the process.'

'So,' she said thoughtfully, 'to go within is to get perspective, to find the still point, the starting place.'

He nodded.

'And you...', her voice trailed off.

'I know how to operate the lever that draws back the curtains. A very simple act, but impossible to accomplish if you don't know where the lever is placed.'

Her eyes gleamed with recognition.

'Simplicity is exactly what I'm beginning to recognise,' she observed. 'Before I met you trying to understand what life was really about just became more and more complicated and more and more confusing. But you brush all the complexity to one side and make me look at everything from a completely different angle.'

'Well that's good that you recognise that Mira. More than anything else the master wants the student to be fulfiled and to see the joy and fun in life. It is a living thing, a journey with a dynamic momentum, in a sense I don't even teach you. I unteach you!'

He laughed.

'It's a process of unlearning all the faulty concepts that are created by focusing too much on the world and on the limitations of the finite self. So now continue on and let's see what is next for you to unlearn!'

Act VI

S he walked on. She came to a clearing. To her left she saw a little house. Two butterflies frolicked in the breeze. Their wings flapped in unison. An old woman appeared in the doorway. She was gnarled and wizened. Her light frame leaned on a walking stick. She looked at Mira through wise grey eyes.

'You are Mira,' she said.

It was a statement rather than a question. Mira nodded.

'I've been expecting you,' she continued beckoning Mira to the open door.

Mira hesitated. She looked behind her to see if he was there. She saw him sauntering along in the distance. She felt reassured and approached the old woman, following her inside. The woman gestured to a seat. Mira sat down.

'You can ask me one question,' the old woman said, sitting heavily into the seat opposite.

Mira felt confused. She didn't really know what this was about or what she could ask. She studied the face of the old woman. She could see that the old lady had once been beautiful. There was a quiet strength and a steely determination in her eyes, a sense that she had been through many of life's adventures and had won through. Almost before she realised it herself a question sprang from her lips.

'What is the bravest thing you have ever done?' she asked the old woman.

The grey eyes grew wistful and gazed at Mira in contemplation.

'I loved, and allowed myself to be loved in return,' the old one replied.

Mira was astounded.

'You mean that of all the things you experienced in your life you really feel that to love and be loved was the bravest?' she said incredulously.

The woman nodded.

'In every other situation there is room for pretence,' she explained. 'You can keep your fears, hopes, inadequacies, and dreams secret, even from yourself. To love is to let another in. They become your mirror and you theirs. There is no longer a secret place because they come to know when you are trying to go there. When love is true you mirror each other equally. You are partners in life.'

She paused, her eyes taking on a faraway look.

'It's not always easy,' she continued. 'It takes hard work and commitment...times of compromise certainly, but compromise is not the same as sacrifice. Love never offers the other as a sacrifice, no matter what the situation.'

She laughed to herself, nodding and smiling as if talking also to an invisible other. Then she looked sharply at Mira. Her tone changed, becoming almost conspiratorial.

'You know exposing the body is not half as frightening as exposing the soul. That is why it is brave. At my age I can look back at all the other joys and pains and they become insignificant with time. What has value is that I can say I was known and I was truly loved for just being who I am. Love is the magic glue that binds all the other bits together. It is the foundation that makes the bad times bearable and the good times perfect.'

The old woman cast a loving glance at a picture on the wall. It was of an elderly man. Her eyes filled with tears.

'He died many years ago,' she said, looking again at the picture.

'But after all you have said about love, how do you go on without him now?' Mira asked.

The woman sighed heavily.

'Oh I won't pretend that I don't miss him every day, but he is in my heart. I learned about life with him not through him. That is the important thing. By allowing him to get to know me I got to know myself and it was the same for him. We were on a journey together but we always knew that a time would come when one of us may have to continue alone. To share your life with someone is just that, it's not a merging of two souls into one. It's two individual souls dancing like sparkles of light on the water, they have a time when they will sparkle on the same pool of water and they have a time when the water ripples and they are pulled apart. To truly love another is to truly love life, and to accept that the time here is precious and temporary. What happens after I don't know, but love is bigger than physical bodies and individual personalities.'

Her eyes twinkled now, flashing a glimpse of the girl she once was.

'Well that's what I think anyway,' she said with a smile. 'Maybe I'm wrong to describe it as brave because in my view it's the only way to live. What's the other option? Waste your time living in fear of getting hurt? Hurts come and go, the memory always fades but I'd go through a thousand hurts if I thought at the end I'd experience the love I experienced even if it was for just a day.'

Mira kissed the old woman softly on the cheek as she left her. Her heart danced. She was beginning to understand that the journey was about love. It was becoming a journey of love, and in love. She saw her relationship with new eyes. She had been distracted from it by her inner travels. She had been viewing it as something separate, now she realised that it was as fragile and precious as the gently butterfly that had landed on her hand. Not something to dissect or pin to a board, but something to just let fly free, yet treasure the fact that it had chosen to fly into her world.

Act VII

When she went outside he was sitting on a rock, dangling his feet in the clear stream that flowed near the house.

'You have a question,' he said raising his eyebrows quizzically, but with the trace of a smile.

'I just met this amazing old woman' she replied. We talked about life and love and I realised that this is all about love. The love I have for my partner and the love I feel inside seem to flow together. I don't know where one stops and the other starts, or even if there should be a separation. Is it all the same?'

'Have you always loved him?' he asked.

'Well I couldn't have,' she answered, 'I didn't always know him.'

'Now you do know him, will you always love him?' he asked.

Mira paused.

'I don't know, I'd like to think I will,' she replied.

'Did you love others before him?' he asked.

'Yes,' she said, 'but not like I love him.'

He laughed heartily.

'Yeah, that's what they all say,' he chortled.

She felt a bit peeved, but bit back a response. She didn't need to say anything, annoyance was written all over her face. He stopped laughing and looked at her gently.

'Don't you see it's all the same?' he continued. 'What you do on the outside is mirrored within. If you can't open your heart to yourself then how can you ever open your heart to others and to a higher love? Fear is fear and if it's there in one part of your life it will flow through and block all the other parts. But,' he said, holding a finger up to make his point, 'there is one big difference between the love of which we speak and the love you have for another, and that is condition.'

She looked confused.

'I don't know what you mean by that,' she said.

'Love between people usually has conditions attached,' he explained. 'You love them and they love you as long as you are treating each other with respect. If one begins to harm the other, if one begins to cause pain in any way to the other the love goes. The love about which I teach is not like that. It was always there and will always be there. I didn't give it to you. I only reminded you that it was there and showed you how to access it. This is not to say that you shouldn't love others openly and fully, it is only to remind you that some love changes while the really true love, the love of the divine, is unchanging and without condition. In life, the tide of emotion ebbs and flows, but this love remains constant. It is the place of calm even when it seems that the storm blows all around.'

'But I love you also, in a way I can't exactly explain, what kind of love is that?' she asked him.

'Who am I?' he asked.

'You are my teacher, my master,' she replied.

He looked away.

'And what are you to me?' he asked.

She thought for a moment and replied, 'I am your student.'

'Ah, the love between master and student' he said with a wry smile, 'that is yet another kind of love.'

He looked at her and his eyes sparkled with a purity that she couldn't describe, but she could feel it as strongly as if it were a solid object.

'I love you and you love me because we are on the same path of love,' he said. 'Our personal lives are not bound together. Nothing binds the student to the master, or the master to the student, except this bond of love. This teaching is from one heart to another and my only interest is in opening your heart. Only in your heart can you know if my teaching has a benefit. What I do in my life has no effect on you as your journey is yours and all I teach you is how to open your own door.

Likewise what you do in your life is of no interest to me. You can be the richest person or the poorest. You can live in a city or on a mountaintop. What you eat, whom you live with, what you believe - all this is irrelevant to the journey within.'

He grew reflective.

'My subject is the appreciation of the gift of life at its simplest, not the 'dos and don'ts' of society. Life is love. Falling in love with life is the greatest thanks you can give in return to that which created this life. My role is to remind you of this, as it is easy to forget. It is easy to become distracted. The master is the signpost, and when you are on a journey is a signpost not the most beautiful sight on the dark road ahead?'

She nodded in agreement.

'Shouldn't everyone have a master then?' she asked.

He shook his head.

'Life is full of choices' he replied. 'This isn't necessarily a path for everyone. Not everyone wants to be taught. Some look at a master and see the master's life and not the master's teaching. They won't necessarily want to live life the way the master does so they reject the whole thing. It's the baby and the bathwater syndrome.'

He paused and tilting his head back looked at her with a twinkle in his eye.

'You know the master very often makes things deliberately difficult. If the master wanted to start a religion or some sort of egotistical attention grabbing campaign then he would say: 'LOOK AT ME! I'M WONDERFUL. I'M JUST WHAT YOU EXPECT ME TO BE'.'

He collapsed in a fit of giggles.

'Then what do you get?' he asked, laughing even harder, tears pouring down his cheeks.

She shook her head.

'You get sheep!' he exclaimed. 'You get people who want to be told what they should believe in.'

He became serious again.

'This is an important point. Blind faith is exactly as it is described – blind. Many wars are fought in the name of love. Well-intentioned people get side-tracked and create their own versions of God then destroy his very creation in the name of whatever version they have chosen.'

He shook his head sadly.

'When the pain gets too unbearable they look to the sky, beat their chests and ask God how he could let them suffer so. But God had nothing to do with it; they did it to themselves because they preferred the fantasy to the reality. They seek outside for something that rests in their own hearts, but because their vision has become so unclear they cannot believe that what they are looking for is within. They look for miracles and signs when the greatest miracle of all, the flow of the breath, is literally right under their noses.'

He stopped and looked at her. Mira had grown sombre as she listened to him.

'You can't fix everyone Mira,' he said gently. 'But you can fix you. You can have peace in your own heart. You can make your own life worthwhile by appreciating every breath, every moment that you are given. What I teach you won't take your problems away. Life is naturally full of ups and downs. But you have a place within that will always give you shelter.'

'Oh Master,' Mira sighed. 'It frustrates me that so much of the pain we cause in the world could be resolved if only we could see the simplicity and not have the tendency to complicate everything. I never tire of listening to you, but you say it is easy to forget. What will happen if I forget? Will you always be my master?'

'It all comes back to love Mira, and to clarity. A true master has understood something about life and has a gift that allows him to pass that understanding on. The understanding is a real experience that can be appreciated only by a student who is willing to look through their own eyes and who can still themselves enough to feel that experience in their own hearts. The true student comes to be taught, not to be led. A master is interested only in that kind of student. The teaching is to remind the student again and again that this life, this breath is the most precious gift. It is human nature to forget and the master understands this, which is why he continues to teach. The true student understands this also, which is why they continue to listen.'

He got up to leave and Mira's eyes followed him. She had only lived a quarter of a century, but she had seen enough to know that he was right. She bent her head and prayed that she would continue to learn to stay focused and clear in the face of whatever might come.

Act VIII

The butterfly flapped its wings. It landed on her heart. She felt a gentle stirring then stillness settled and love washed through her. She savoured its sweetness. She became aware of herself almost peeping out from within her own being. She opened her eyes. He was sitting on the grass and had a large birdcage in front of him.

He turned to her.

'Mira, come take a look at this sad little bird!' he said softly.

In the cage was a beautiful songbird, but it was silent and withdrawn.

'What's wrong with it?' she asked.

'It was rescued by a friend of mine,' he replied. 'It was kept in a dark room and has never been out of the cage. It has never learned to fly or to sing. My friend nursed it back to health, but he can't get it to come out of its own free will. He leaves the cage door open, but the bird isn't interested. Even when he takes it out of the cage the bird runs back in as soon as it can. So, he asked me to help.'

He shook his head sadly.

'It's a classic,' he murmured, almost to himself,

'caged for so long that the desire for freedom has been forgotten.'

'What will you do?' she asked.

He took the bird out and cradled it in his hands. She could see that the bird's heart was beating quickly. Its body trembled in fear.

'I'll tell you both a story' he said with a smile, 'then I'll teach this bird to fly.'

Holding the bird gently he began.

'Once upon a time there was a little drop. The little drop lived on a very big and solid rock right out in the middle of the vast blue ocean.

Little Drop sat on the rock and said: 'This is my world.'

Little Drop sat on the rock and said: 'This is my nature.'

Little Drop sat on the rock and said: 'I am solid. I am just like the rock. I will endure.'

But Little Drop was not rock, and though it searched and searched it could not find a way to make itself feel hard as rock. It could not find a way to stay solid instead of crystal clear. It pushed itself into tiny crevices and waited to see if time would freeze it there. It lay out flat along the surface, hoping that the rock would soak it in. It asked the shellfish to let it sit near them to learn how it could hang there just like them. But nothing worked, and Little Drop grew larger from its tears.

Then the ocean lapped towards the rock, and called to the Little Drop to join it. But Little Drop pulled back and said: 'I have no need of you. I am on this solid rock. You are just formless sea. You are not like me!'

Time passed, and Little Drop was not content. Try as it might it could not find a way to make itself become solid like the rock.

And the ocean lapped again. It said: 'Little Drop, can you not see that all the while I chip away at this great rock. It is I who makes the sand. It is I who took the sand and formed it into this giant rock.'
But the Little Drop scoffed: 'I do not believe you. You who are so shapeless, how could you shape?'

Time passed and the Little Drop grew anxious. It could feel its strength fading. As it searched for a place in the rock, the sun beat down melting parts of Little Drop away.

And the ocean lapped again. It said: 'Little Drop, come join me now! If you do not, soon the sun will have melted you away, and it will take a long, long time before you become a Little Drop again.'

The Little Drop began to listen. It could see the sun carrying other drops very far away. It could see new drops appear and search for ways to be like the rock. It could see rocks crumbling into dust. The Little Drop grew uncertain. It looked out to the ocean, and wished that it could be as big and powerful as that vast sea.

And the ocean lapped again. And the Little Drop wanted proof that it would feel as solid as the rock if it joined with the ocean. But the ocean shook its head. It said: 'Little Drop, I can give you no such proof. I am not of rock, but nor are you, for you are not rock but sea.'

The Little Drop was doubtful. It wondered: 'How could something as little as me have anything at all to do with that vast sea?'

All around the Little Drop more and more of the other drops were beginning to disappear and, noticing this, the Little Drop forgot its fear. It trickled from its rock towards the ocean.

The Little Drop was finally in the sea. It lay quietly for a moment, thinking, 'Any moment now I'll fade into the sea.' But something strange began to happen. The Little Drop could feel what it was like to be of water. It could feel solidity of a different sort. It could feel the giant form that is the ocean, and all the while its little self did not disappear.

The Little Drop sparkled with delight. It could feel the sun but did not fear it. It was part of something magical, which would not disappear. It saw the little rock, and saw the difference between rock and sea. It rippled out and felt its hugeness. It asked the ocean:

'How could it be I thought I was rock? Why did you let me sit there thinking I was different from the sea?'

The ocean lapped in laughter. 'Why Little Drop I put you on the rock so that you could feel the difference. So that you would search for your own feeling and that one day you would return knowing who you are. So that you could understand, that being part of me does not mean the end of you. So that you would see that one little drop was ocean all along."

As he finished the story he looked at her, waiting for her reaction.   Mira's eyes glistened with tears.

'That is such a beautiful story,' she whispered.

He nodded.

'It's a very simple story that contains a very profound truth,' he said quietly.

He held his hand over the bird's heart. The bird was rested and still. Its chest no longer trembled and heaved. It turned its head and looked trustingly into the brown eyes that smiled down on it.

'The world can give all the theories of how to be. I give the feeling. That is the nature of what a master teaches. Showing this bird the open door is not enough. It has to feel trust. Only then will it feel its own power, its own nature. It may not understand the words I am speaking but it can feel my language.'

He stood up and held his hands to the sky. The bird flew. It flew hesitantly and unsteadily. Its wings were weak, but still it flew. Mira held her breath, afraid to move a muscle in case she would frighten it. The bird landed, after circling him once, and came back to him. It was tired, but there was a confidence in its walk. He picked it up and put it back in the cage.

'A first step,' he said smiling, 'but the most important one. From this point of trust and courage, the rest will follow.'

Mira thought about the bird as she walked on.

'People ask how you know if a master is truly a master,' she thought to herself. 'I wish they could have seen that. He so reeks of the experience within that it's almost tangible. Even that little bird felt it.'

She was filled with a bubble of happiness that she could feel it too. She giggled to herself as she walked along, conjuring up news stories in her head:

ONE SMALL STEP FOR BIRDKIND
One Giant Leap For A Little Unknown Songbird!

Today a songbird flew for the first time following three years in solitary confinement.

The bird commented "I didn t know I could fly. I was given to believe that the cage was part of my body. I m thrilled of course to find out that I was wrong."

57

Act IX

She continued on. The path narrowed and ahead she could see a tunnel. Her footsteps faltered a little, as she was unable to see what lay on the other side. She took a deep breath and made her way towards it.

'If a little bird can overcome a fear of the unknown then so can I,' she muttered to herself.

The tunnel was roughly hewn out of the rocky hillside. It was dark and featureless. As she passed through she could smell dampness and could hear the soft rhythmic plop of water dripping from some unseen crevice. She reached the other side and surveyed the territory ahead. The scene was bleak. In front of her was a sweeping grey plain. Wind swirled and eddied. Its low moan filled her with a heart-wrenching sadness, making her feel utterly alone.

She became aware of a low rumbling sound behind her. It was quickly followed by a deafening crash. Startled she jumped out of the path of the noise, but when she looked behind her, there was nothing there. She retraced her footsteps back into the tunnel to see where the noise had come from. She was met by a wall of high rocks and a billowing cloud of dust. Part of the roof of the tunnel had collapsed and now the path back was blocked. She felt a lump rise in her throat as the realisation dawned on her that there was no way back.

'Now stay calm,' she said to herself, turning again to walk back to the desolate plain.

The expanse of grey stretched outward, broken only by a dark mountain, looming in the distance to her right. It rose up from the plain in a great mound. It wasn't connected to anything in particular. It was just there, a solitary monolithic shape beckoning her to come closer.

Night was falling and she needed shelter so she walked towards the mountain. As she got nearer, the sheer scale of its hugeness filled her with trepidation. In its crevices shadows seemed to break and sigh. She noticed that one shadow seemed deeper than the rest. It was a cave. She went towards it and went inside. Shivering, she tried to fight off all thoughts of what insects could be creeping and crawling in its depths. She huddled in the corner and, hugging her knees to her chest, sat as close to the rocky wall as she could. 'At least it's warm,' she thought, trying to cheer herself up.

Thunder rolled overhead and the rain began to pour down in driving sheets. Every flash of lightening made her jump and, each time it struck, it lit the cave for an instant giving the impression that strange shapes and forms were darting about its depths. She closed her eyes tightly, in an attempt to block out the reality of being in this dark place. It didn't really work. She began to cry. The words of a Suzanne Vega song she hadn't heard for years kept repeating in her head - *Solitude stands by the doorway. I m struck once again by her dark silhouette, her long cool stare and her silence..* The empty cave soon filled with the sound of her sobs.

Eventually she fell asleep. She began to dream. In her dream she was standing in the mouth of the cave looking out on the grey plain. She was searching for light. She was sure it was out there, an unseen oasis, surrounded by the potboil grey, the pit of night. She stood, arms outstretched clawing at the greyness, face tilted to the driving rain. A figure appeared in front of her. She recognised the figure. It was the Being of Light whom she had met before. The Being started to speak in a strange keening voice. She was reciting a poem by Yeats:

> *Turning and turning in the widening gyre.*
> *The falcon cannot hear the falconer;*
> *Things fall apart; the centre cannot hold;*
> *Mere anarchy is loosed upon the world*

The words floated.

She stopped reciting and looked at Mira. Mira returned her gaze.

'Absence becomes a soother, a concrete thing, that you can feel such loss, that you can feel...' the Being whispered.

The words floated.

The Being shook her head. Her voice lilted on.
'Why are you looking out?
Have you forgotten something?'

Mira sat bolt upright, banging her head on the rock wall.

'Oh my God!' she thought to herself, rubbing her head distractedly, 'how could I have forgotten the most basic thing? I can feel! I can feel because I'm alive and now I'm wasting precious time on fear! The poem is wrong. The centre can hold. The centre always holds. We just forget!'

She realised that her problem was trust. She wasn't trusting that she could feel at peace regardless of the situation. Realising that the problem was trust, and not loneliness or fear of being alone, consoled her. Now she had something she could focus on. She needed to look at the positive in this situation. Time alone was an opportunity, a chance to really take another step on her path. She was beginning to understand the importance of perseverance.

She closed her eyes.

'I need to look within,' she murmured to herself.

She felt the stillness settle. The sense of isolation welled up and she felt it almost engulf her again.

'I can get out of here,' she said to herself over and over again, 'because I'm not anywhere.'

She refused to follow the feeling of despair and felt herself float through it. With every breath she went further in. It felt as though she was passing through layers of emotion. Old memories of hurts and arguments flickered past, like images on a TV screen, but she remained detached. She saw her actions, her needs, her insecurities and noticed how they fed off the needs and insecurities of others. They became insubstantial, like projections that dissolved at a touch.

As she travelled through the levels of feeling she felt herself arrive at the point of stillness. It flowed gently in and out. It was calm and removed from all the layers above it. Silence fell. She felt peace settle. The storm passed. The wind died down. Grey clouds rolled back to make way for a shaft of sunlight. It brushed against her forehead, then travelled slowly to her heart. She felt its warmth. She opened her eyes. Dancing eyes looked into hers. Her heart fluttered in recognition. He was there. He smiled at her.

'You're here!' she exclaimed. 'I thought I was all alone.'

Her voice lowered.

'I was really frightened at first. Despite all you have taught me, I felt panicked,' she whispered. 'I felt very far away and I thought you were gone.'

'What have you learned?' he asked.

She was thoughtful.

'I saw that all the things that cause me pain are insubstantial. It's like we all throw images and impressions at each other when at the core of everything we are all coming from the same feeling of love and compassion. I can see the tendency to latch on to the immediate reaction without looking at what is really going on. And finding myself here, at first I did it again. I was swallowed by the sad feelings and forgot that I could try to get beyond them. I forgot that I could do this for myself.'

'I hadn't left you,' he said gently, 'but you can only see me when your eyes are clear and your ears are stilled enough to hear your heart speak. The heart feels no chaos. Its drumbeat is simplicity. Its desire is to be in love and to feel no duality. It is the happiness of contentment. Chaos lives in the mind, in the nerves, in the sinews. It feeds on turbulent emotions, on the rapid firing of agitated brain cells; it battles against the simple calm of the soul. The dark night of the soul lives in the mind. Only the mind can create the very traps that lead it to self-destruct.'

'But even though I know that the love is there, still I forgot, still sorrow and despair crept in,' she remarked.

He looked pensive.

'As the quote goes - 'where light is brightest, shadows are deepest',' he replied. 'It has a truth. The path of the heart is often a lonely path, of tests, trials and initiations. Each soul carves its own path. The love is always there. Until that recognition dawns, the battles will rage. This may not be your last but you are learning. Stay vigilant. Let no room for doubt in your heart. The heart is never off course. Trust in that.'

Act X

He took her hand.

The butterfly wings flapped again. They were of the deepest purple and as the butterfly flew upwards shards of violet and indigo dust poured from its wingtips.

The world shifted. It dissolved. All that was left were interconnecting lines of light and energy. She heard the hum. She had heard that before. But now it was as if the hum had a structure and was the fabric from which everything was formed. He was standing next to her, his eyes shining with love as he watched the scene before them. It was a spiralling dance of light and movement.

'Remember what I told you about looking and seeing,' he murmured.

She nodded. She slowed her breath so that it became deep and calm and allowed her eyes to just relax. She became very still. She looked again. It was as if her eyes had become microscopes as she could see the tiny elements that made up the dance. As she continued to focus she saw that the scene was full of people. Millions of figures were flowing and whirling in individual streams of light and colour. He took her hand and they began to walk amongst the dancing figures closest to them.

She gasped as she realised that they were all parts of her. They each danced in their own spheres and she saw that there were many paths leading from sphere to sphere. Some were direct, some meandered off into vast spirals leading away through darkened spaces and shadow-lands before coming back to the doorway to the next sphere. She saw how the paths were chosen. It depended on whether the dancer's eyes were open or closed and on what part of the dance was completed. She saw the patterns. Her past selves shut their eyes tight when the dance became difficult. The path then chosen invariably led into a slowed down variation. But until the eyes opened and all steps of the dance were completed, the path could not be escaped.

She blinked and looked again. Now she could see many others, besides her, dancing in their spheres. Some were stuck and were dancing the same path over and over, their eyes firmly shut. Some had stopped and were refusing to dance and their spheres were shrivelling around them. Some danced effortlessly from sphere to sphere, their eyes bright and open, always alert to the point in the sphere that led to the clearest path.

She slowed her thoughts and she saw the entire dance

of the universe. The colours poured down and interconnected and circled. She saw that everything was one. Everything had meaning and nothing was isolated. She saw the butterfly and saw its heart was her heart. She saw that the infinite was as present in a fragment as it was in the whole. She saw that there were no accidents or coincidences only synchronicities. She saw that she had been in the dance for the longest time and that the dance was more substantial than the world she knew. More than anything else she felt one with all she saw. Then she felt herself move back and, once again, she was looking into the smiling eyes. She was herself again.

'Well,' he said playfully, 'did you like that?'

'It's the most beautiful thing I've ever experienced,' she replied. 'But all the versions I saw just of me, not to mention all the millions and millions of others…'

She paused and grew pensive.

'It's a pattern isn't it?' she continued. 'I got the sense that everything is interconnected and yet choice still exists.'

He nodded.

'Yes, there is connection, there is a pattern. The beauty is that from within you can see the pattern. The wheel turns. Good things come, then they go. Bad things come, then they go. That is the nature of life.

Forever moving, forever turning. The rules within are different. That is where the connection is felt. Within, the flow is always upwards, always constant, always in bliss. Without the knowledge of the self within, then the constant grind of the wheel can become a trap. Looking at it from within, however, lets you see that there are two processes going on. The bigger picture I suppose you could say. Knowing the bigger picture gives you the tools to get out of the grind of the wheel. It opens the eyes.'

'It's to be conscious isn't it?' she asked.

He nodded.

'It's so difficult at times,' she continued. 'Like in the cave, the fear and isolation knocked me right into an unconscious process.'

'But you kept trying Mira,' he said. 'That is the most important lesson. You are human. There are times when you will get knocked and will fall down, when you will feel that the connection with the heart is lost. It's in knowing that you have fallen and in making the effort to get up again the importance lies. It's an onward journey. Pick yourself up, dust yourself down, learn from it and don't look back. Nothing is more fruitless than regret.'

Act XI

She was resting, basking in the sunshine and thinking dreamily about the beauty of the spheres.

The butterflies circled overhead. They seemed to be having a conversation. They fluttered purposefully and came to rest on the brim of an ornate silver cup. They put their heads together and seemed to peer inside. They bobbed up again and were lost in discussion. Then silence fell and each began to have a gentle giggle. Still laughing they rose upwards and flew away, their myriad colours trailing after them on the breeze.

She opened her eyes. She was in a white room. It was full of computers and electronic gadgets. She could hear the whir of the equipment. She felt something on her head. She touched it and, to her amazement, felt a cap of wires and little electrodes just sitting there. A tall man in a white coat appeared in front of her. He was making notes on a page attached to clipboard in his hand.

'Where am I?' she asked, sounding irritated.

'Oh don't worry,' he said briskly. 'We're measuring brain activity in people who meditate. Taking scans of the Godspot as we call it.'

Mira looked astonished.

'You think you can see a Godspot!' she exclaimed incredulously.

He nodded. He brought her over a series of scans.

'You see this is what we are finding,' he explained holding up a colourful scan.

He pointed to a picture of red blobs on a background of yellow.

'This is the brain in a normal waking state.'

Then he held up the second scan. This time the picture had the same structure but the bottom right corner was plain yellow with very little red.

'This is you in deep meditation.'

Pointing at the first scan he said: 'In this reality the self is firmly separate from the world around it. We call it the parietal lobe. It is the area which orientates experience and gives the person the sense of their own self, separate from the world around them.'

He held up the second scan and indicated the yellow patch.

'Here, when meditating, the blood flow, which shows neural activity, is reduced. This leads to a breakdown in feelings of separation and leads to an experience of oneness of self and non-self.'

He stopped and looked smugly satisfied. Mira looked at

him expectantly.

'And?' she said.

'And what?' he replied.

'Is that it? I mean is that as far as you've got?'

He looked indignant.

'What do you mean 'is that it'! This is very significant research.'

She bit her lip, trying to think of a less confrontational way to approach him.

'I mean,' she continued slowly, 'it's one thing to see these things on a scan and to understand that this leaves a physical trace in the brain, but it is quite another to be able to understand why the ability is there.'

He looked frustrated.

'But it shows that both states are as real as each other because both exist. These scans prove that they do.'

Mira sighed.

'Isn't that what all the great teachers have been saying for millennia. You may not want to listen to them because they're not scientific, but your results depend on them. Without their teaching there would be no subjects to measure because no one would know how to do it. Furthermore, your scans will never be able to tell you why we can do it.'

The room dissolved and all she could hear was the

sound of laughter. She looked around and saw her master lying on the ground holding his stomach, tears pouring from his eyes, and his body shaking with peals of laughter.

'Did you just see all that?' she asked him crossly. 'They had electrodes on me measuring my Godspot!'

Suddenly the silliness of the situation hit her too and she began to laugh.

'It brings a whole new meaning to G-spot doesn't it!' she giggled.

Finally they sat up and looked at each other.

'So where was the lesson in that?' she asked.

'There wasn't one really' he chuckled. 'I just thought it would tickle that inquiring mind of yours to see that science was catching on. It's all very eleventh dimension. It runs rings around them, like quantum particles dashing around saying 'can't catch me-ee'.'

She looked at him curiously.

'What do you mean by 'very eleventh dimension'?' she asked.

'Oh I don't talk about that, I just breathe it,' he replied nonchalantly.

Realising that he was teasing her she affected an impressed look and took a deep breath.

'Now I've had some too!' she joked as she exhaled heavily.

'Lucky us,' he said, winking at her. 'Let's do that for a while.'

They both spent some time happily focusing on their breaths, until she broke the silence.

'I'm not anti-science you know,' she said with a mischievous look. 'Like quantum realities and things, I really like that stuff.'

'I know you do,' he said with a smirk. 'That's why I thought that deep down you'd quite enjoy the idea of the scans.'

He sat back and folded his arms.

'I know you're dying to talk about this so go on, tell me about the life of a quantum particle,' he said, his eyes dancing with mirth.

'All right then,' she smiled, knowing that he was indulging her, 'what do you want to know?'

'Just how they work" he replied.

'Well, I'm not a physicist,' she said in her most scientific voice, 'but I'll do my best.'

'You see,' she continued, 'the quantum world is not bound by the same laws as the actual visible and tangible world we see around us. In this visible world, the nature of things is an entropic one; meaning that all things proceed naturally from a state of order to one of disorder.'

'Meaning, in normal language,' he interjected, 'that

all things, including people, age, die and decay. Buildings crumble, metals corrode, landscapes erode?'

She nodded.

'Yes,' she agreed, 'but for the quantum particle it's different. It doesn't go in a logical direction of order to disorder. It tries everything at the same time and always leaves a trace. Like, for example, when you're buying a house, you look at a few, then pick one and move in. That's not how the quantum particle would do it. It would move into all of them, trying each simultaneously. All the neighbours in the different neighbourhoods would remember this particle that moved in next door. When it would finally decide on the house it wanted, all its other selves would leave the other houses but all the neighbours in the different neighbourhoods would still remember the particle that lived next door – that's what leaving a trace means.'

He clapped his hands.

'Very good!' he exclaimed.

'It is interesting though isn't it,' she commented. 'I think it's all quite magical.'

'Well you don't have to look very far to see all of that at work,' he said. 'It's not unlike us you know. Passion comes along, hits you in the face, you're blown out of your steady state to go and experience it and if you're not careful, stability is forgotten, consciousness is forgotten. Passion can have many forms - a relationship, an ambition, a job, a religion, an addiction even - and having the experience might not be a bad thing in itself. It's letting it take over that creates the pain, both for yourself and for others. To be unconscious is not to be asleep; it is to be unaware. In the unconscious state emotions leak out in all directions, gnawing at your own self and affecting and impacting on anyone who may be at the receiving end of your lack of clarity.'

'Mmm..,' she murmured thoughtfully, 'I hadn't thought of emotions like that before.'

He nodded.

'Physical life goes with the physical laws but consciousness is more like your quantum particle, always striving for the stable position. Two realities, two worlds - one which can be seen and touched, and the other which can only be felt. But the feeling within is even more powerful. It has a direct connection to the divine.'

'How do we know that the inner feeling is connected to the divine? How do we know that it's not just an aspect of brain chemistry, like the good doctor was trying to imply?' she asked.

He looked pensive.

'Something allows an inner evolution to become possible. Something within pushes for growth;

something within broke free of the order to disorder cycle. Something within allows a physical body to feel an intangible realm. I call that divine.'

'So,' she said slowly, 'we have our physical selves, our quantum-like consciousness and, at our core, a spark of something beyond both, a spark of the divine.'

He nodded.

'Now was all of that in your scan?' he asked her with a smirk.

'It sure beats a yellow blob,' she quipped, and they both shook with laughter again.

Act XII

Still smiling to herself and aware that somewhere in her mind there was a little part of her still chasing scans and quantum particles, she continued on.

She came to a beach. The sand was golden and warm so she took off her shoes and padded along towards the water's edge. The water was surprisingly cold but it felt good. She paddled in the water enjoying the feeling of the wavelets breaking against her legs. After a while she returned to the beach. She found a quiet spot and sat down to sunbathe. She thought about all that had happened on her journey thus far and realised that her life had completely altered. Days went as they had gone before, filled with work, social outings, family get-togethers and so on, but everything was different. The sense of something else was now so present that it was tangible. The old familiarity of what she used to call 'everydayness' was replaced with the sense that the pulse of life was everywhere and it was a pulse that moved to a different beat.

A butterfly flitted over her head. It flapped its wings. There was a downpour of colour. She felt sleepy. She closed her eyes and felt an explosion of warmth flow from her stomach to her heart. In a flutter of light the Being materialised. She shimmered and glowed.

'You've done well,' she smiled. 'You know who I am. Now it's time that our eyes were one. I see in all directions and in all dimensions. You sense my power but now it is time to become conscious of it.'

The Being kissed her on the forehead. Mira felt that she was falling.

'I'm like Alice going down, down the rabbit hole,' she thought dreamily.

Space fell away. She felt herself expand in all directions.

'Knowledge of the self is not a static thing,' the Being said, her voice floating somewhere in Mira's head. 'A point comes when the knowledge within begins to teach the knowledge within. Like endlessly reflecting mirrors, the perspective becomes infinite. You will do the learning; he will keep you clear. This is a time for humility. When you feel that you might not need him any more is the time you will need him most.'

The voice was gone, but Mira felt different. She could feel the power coursing through her. She looked around her. She gazed at the ocean. It was a beautiful view. A clear horizon stretching far out to sea, white waves crashing on the shore and the bluest water she had ever seen. The warm breeze caressed her skin. Everything around her had an added vibrancy. She could see the dance of the spheres superimposed on the physical world around her. The two merged and became one. A glow of life seemed to surround every pebble, every wave, every shard of sunlight rippling on the water. She wanted to shout at all the people walking on the beach to tell them that they were all magical beings. It was as if she could see what was going on in their hearts. The minutiae of their lives seemed to sing from their eyes. She could sense their joys, their sorrows, their worries, their hopes and their fears. She saw what a gift it was to be human.

'Everyone is so different' she thought to herself, 'yet we all move to the same beat. In our hearts we all have the same longing, the same beauty.'

She thought of the story her master told about the little drop and smiled to herself.

'I feel like that little drop now as it got its first taste of what it really means to be part of the ocean,' she said to herself with a deep sigh of satisfaction. 'I've often read about the scales being lifted from the eyes, and I never really understood it, but that is exactly what this feels like!'

She sat on the beach for what seemed like an

eternity, entranced by her heightened perception of all the sights and sounds that surrounded her.

Act XIII

She eventually left the beach and wandered on. As she meandered along enthralled by the vibrancy of everything she could see, she began to notice that here and there the vibrancy dimmed. Perhaps dimmed was the wrong word, it was more a sense that the light at times imploded inward, then dissolved into the warm air. She concentrated her gaze at one dissolving light and saw that it surrounded a frail butterfly resting quietly on a rock. It was very still. As the colours around it began to fade and dissolve she realised what was happening. The butterfly was dying. She sat quietly by the butterfly and felt profoundly moved to be with it during its last moments of life.

Her heart became heavy. She remembered the first time she saw death. It was in her grandfather's eyes. His face was white with fear, as he frantically clutched her grandmother's hand. His mouth was a rumble of mutterings. He had death in his expression. He had final knowledge in his soul. The recognition of death and the inability to express it, such was the nature of his stroke. This was how she saw him for the last time, convulsing against the confines of finality. She was seven years old. As she remembered it, she had hysterics and went to bed. According to her mother she did not react. She had just stood there as if she didn't understand. But she did understand. There was something he had not grasped about life and in those final moments, she saw that realisation dawn in his eyes. The memory had never left her. She realised now that this is what had shaped her desire to really understand what life meant.

Her master stood next to her quietly watching the butterfly.

'And it was going so beautifully until time came knocking,' he said.

'The understanding you have given me about how precious this gift of life is has made death all the more painful. Even to watch this butterfly die is heartbreaking, and yet every moment somebody somewhere in the world dies. The sad thing is that I realise we have become so used to hearing about tragedies and death tolls that it seems to me that we are becoming immune. We discuss how terrible it is for a while, then shrug our shoulders and move on to the next news item.'

'Yes, that's very often how it is,' he replied. 'Every so often something happens to shock us out of our complacency, then time passes, we forget and life returns to normal again. However, understanding the gift of life means that each time you hear of a death then you won't just casually cast it aside, nor will you die with it. Instead you will appreciate even more that something as fragile as the breath continues to flow in your own life.'

'What happens when we die?' she asked.

He laughed.

'Why do you want to know? Are you planning on dying?' he asked lightly, registering her obvious irritation.

'No, I'm really asking,' she insisted. 'What happens when we die?'

'Seriously though,' he continued, 'you need to look at what is behind that question. You were born and one day you will die. These are certain things. Life is the space in between. While you're here your focus must be on that space. Why let your focus wander from that space? How are you filling it?'

'But that's my question,' she said in frustration, 'if I'm to fill it doesn't it imply that I'm filling it for a reason?'

He laughed and shook his head.

'Oh the mind, the mind it always seeks to take you through empty corridors full of doors that lead you to empty rooms.'

He looked at her sternly, but in seeing her genuine confusion his gaze softened.

'Where were you before you were born?' he asked.

'I've no idea,' she replied.

'But you're here aren't you. Something took care of you. Something set it up so that you'd arrive in a safe womb. You weren't in control in the womb either were you?'

She shook her head.

'The difference between you then and you now is trust. Then you had to trust that it would all be taken care of and it was. Why should you think that you wouldn't be taken care of in the future? The whole point of having the inner experience is to feel the difference between the finite and the infinite so that you can appreciate and trust what has been being given to you.'

She told him about her grandfather and how it didn't seem to her that death was easy for him or a process that led him to any sense of inner recognition or trust.

'That's a big assumption,' he said.

'What is?' she asked.

'To assume that you could know what was happening in his heart. Perhaps he didn't reach an understanding, perhaps he did. You'll never know. Maybe what you saw at that time was just a reflection of your own uncertainty.'

She nodded, almost to herself, realising that he was

right.

'All this time', she said hesitantly, 'I held that assumption about how he felt. But of course you're right. That may have been how his initial reaction appeared to me, but I don't know and can't know how it was for him at the very end. Look even at how I reacted...I thought I had taken it very badly. The bad reaction is what I remember but my mother says I showed no trace of upset and so everyone assumed I was too young to really understand what I had seen. That alone should teach me that we can never know what anyone is really feeling.'

'Well whatever he did or didn't feel is not something you can influence, so you have to let go of it or else your assumption and your interpretation of what you saw then will continue to influence you.'

'I don't understand what you mean by that', she said.

'You saw a part of one person's process', he replied. 'There is always choice. You can choose to be swallowed by fear or you can choose to remove yourself from the control of fear. Did your Grandfather have the ability to make that choice when it counted? I don't know. Do you have the ability to make that choice? Yes, because you are choosing to learn now about the process of living consciously. And, to finally answer your question, what you take with you is your consciousness.'

He continued: 'If your consciousness isn't used to feeling at one with its infinite nature, then how do you think it will suddenly learn to do that when the moment comes for the finite to separate from the infinite? Separation will come, that I can guarantee. Where it leads I refuse to speculate. I'm not dead and I haven't met any dead people.'

He grew serious again.

'But remember one thing Mira, above all else, even in your darkest hour you are not abandoned. Be clear on what makes a darkest hour though. It's not the stuff that life can throw at you. It's when you forget the experience within, when you forget to trust that what you seek is within. What you give out you get back so let trust and clarity flow not fear, nor doubt, nor confusion. Do you understand?'
Mira nodded and took a deep breath.

'Life is for the living Mira. Respect the process of coming and going. Welcome those who arrive and mourn those who have left. In remaining conscious you can support those close to you in learning about what it means to be here and in learning to trust the process of leaving. But waste no time in worrying about the inevitable. Just ensure that you are filling your own cup of conscious experience so that, when your time comes, you, in turn, will remain in that place of trust and stillness.'

Act XIV

Come with me,' he said holding out his hand.

She took his hand and they walked along the sandy dunes that overlooked the ocean. Sea grasses flowed and rippled in the wind while, below them, the vast blueness seemed to stretch to infinity. A cool sea breeze rolled across the dunes. Its salt smell filled her nostrils with a refreshing tang.

'All is in perfect balance here,' he said smiling. 'The grasses hold the dunes and the dunes hold the ocean.'

They sat down on a grassy patch and drank in the wild beauty of their surroundings.

'In the realm of this life balance is necessary,' he continued. 'It reminds me of the story about the leaderless kingdom.'

'I don't know that story. Will you tell me?' she asked.

He nodded and began.

"Once there was a beautiful kingdom. The kingdom was abundant with all the riches needed to support its people. The King was a wise man but had no family. He had ruled wisely and fairly and had ensured that everyone shared equally in the riches of his kingdom.

When he knew that his time was short he worried about what might happen to his people. He knew that those around him hungered for power and that they would seek to seize the riches for themselves. One day while walking in the woods pondering his problem he met a wise woman who possessed the gift of magic. She saw that he was troubled and asked him what worried him so. He told her of his fears and she thought for a while then placed her hand on his heart.

'Yes,' she said to him, 'I can see that your heart is true. I know how to resolve your dilemma.'

She brought him back to her humble cottage and asked him to pluck a hair from his head. He gave her the hair and she placed it in a loom. Then she asked him to prick his finger and, when he did so, she took a drop of blood and placed it on top of the hair. She took his hand and closed her eyes as she recited a charm over the loom. The loom began to weave with lightening speed and soon the richest purple cloth flowed to the floor. She picked up the cloth and said:

'I will make a royal coat from this cloth. The moment you pass away all the seals to your treasury will close. Your kingdom will continue as if you are still there and people will be provided for, as you would wish, for one year. For a new King to take your place he will have to provide a golden lining for this coat. The coat will bond only with the purest lining. Once the coat and its lining come together the wearer of the cloak will become King and the treasury will open. If the year ends and no King is found then the treasury will remain closed forever and your people will have to build their wealth from scratch.'

He took the coat and returned to his palace and told his courtiers what had been agreed. Soon after the King passed away.

In a little village far from the palace a little boy played in the fields. Everyday he spent hours watching the plants and animals, marvelling at the many ways nature had of surviving and flourishing. His mother was pleased to see the love her son had for all living things and gave him some ground for himself to make a garden. He loved all plants, but most of all he loved sunflowers and would spend hours watching them as they slowly turned their yellow faces to follow the sun. He decided to plant sunflowers in his patch of ground. For months he tended his seeds and when the flowers were grown he would run to see them every morning, his eyes sparkling with delight that they were growing so well.

One morning when he went to his bed of flowers they had been vandalised. They lay on the ground broken and trampled. He cried and cried as he removed the dead flowers and lovingly re-staked the flowers that were still living. When he had finished he sat holding the dead flowers wondering how anyone could be so cruel. Suddenly a cloud of golden light appeared before him. The gold shimmered and he saw that it was an angel.

The angel spoke saying: 'I am the Angel of the Sunflowers. I have seen your love grow day by day and now I see your pain as you are exposed to the cruel truth that there are those in this world that will recklessly destroy. Because your reaction was to restore and not to seek retribution I wish to reward you.'

The angel bent down and took the dead flowers from the boy's hands. He ran his hands over the flowers and they seemed to melt at his touch. Then he held his hands out to the boy and the boy saw the most beautiful golden coat materialise. It was woven with sunflower petals and though it looked fragile as sunlight it was a strong as a suit of armour. He put it on and it was a perfect fit. The boy was thrilled.

The angel spoke again: 'Far from here is the King's palace. You are to go there now. The reason will become apparent when you arrive.'

The boy and his mother set off and soon arrived at the palace. In the palace there was chaos. There were only ten days left before the year-end and the courtiers had searched far and wide for someone with a lining that could match the coat. People came with coats woven from gold filament, with coats made from the finest silks, with coats embroidered with delicate golden crystals and yet nothing had worked. As they mingled in the crowd outside the palace the little boy's mother heard the story of the royal purple coat. She gasped as she realised why the angel had sent them to the palace and was worried at what this would mean for her son. However she knew that she had to trust what would come if this was the path that was meant for him, so she pushed her way to the palace gates. When they saw that here was yet another golden coat they let her through. The courtiers brought out the purple coat and the little boy slipped it on over his golden coat. With a sparkle of light the two coats merged and the keys to the treasury appeared in the boy's hand.

The courtiers were outraged.

'How can a young child run this kingdom!' shouted one. 'What does he know? He is a country boy!' shouted another.

Suddenly the thud of a large stick banging on the marble resounded through the throne room and all fell silent. It was the wise woman. She told them who she was, then walked towards the boy and placed her hand on his heart. She paused for a while, then smiled and nodded. She said to them: 'When I wove this purple coat I wove into it the wisdom of the King and all who had ruled before him. This coat will impart wisdom to the wearer but it cannot give a pure heart. This boy may be a child but he has a true heart and an unselfish love. His heart will always lead him to the right decisions and the coat will teach him the wisdom he will require. With this balance of wisdom and love he will prove to be a strong and fair ruler.'

The courtiers were sorry for what they had said and in the years that followed, as the kingdom went from strength to strength, they were very thankful for the wise young King that ruled them."

'Now, that's a nice story isn't it?' he said.

She nodded in agreement.

'I can imagine why they would have been so worried about their future King being a mere child. I don't think that in reality many countries would be happy to have a young child as the supreme decision maker. But I can see from my own journey that my greatest understanding comes when I try to view things with the simplicity and willingness to embrace learning that I had as a child.'

'Well that's the point of the story,' he replied. 'Not to revert to childhood, but to hold true to the openness and innocence of childhood. Concepts are just man made constructs. A good heart and the ability to understand wise direction are not the product of years but the product of a balanced approach. In this case the child, through learning well from the lessons nature taught him and through following his heart, responded wisely to adversity. He trusted the higher spirit and accepted its direction without question, even though it meant that he had to journey into the unknown and for an undisclosed reason. This is just a story, but what it teaches is that wisdom is always there. The logic and intellect can learn from age-old wisdom very quickly, but if the heart is not speaking with equal clarity then a true understanding of how to apply the wisdom is impossible.'

'Balance then is integration really,' she posited. 'It's to listen to the voice of the heart but to also remember that the intellect has its own valuable strengths?'

'Yes,' he said. 'The intellect and the heart should not be in opposition. They should be united in a common effort to live life to its fullest and in a way that resolves duality. It is no good to devote special time to the heart and develop a rich inner life, while using the intellect in the day to day world to cheat or deceive.'

'Like when you hear people say it doesn't matter if it's wrong because this world is an illusion anyway?' she asked.

'Exactly,' he nodded. 'This world may be temporary, but the infinite resides in everyone and everyone is linked by that infinite presence. To hurt anyone is to hurt everyone, including the person that is doing the hurting. I'm not talking here about man-made laws – they vary from culture to culture. But the law of the heart is the same in every living being and it has only one rule: to live consciously and in appreciation of the amazing gift that is life.'

Mira smiled.

'It all sounds so simple, and yet it's not as easy to really put it into practice all the time,' she said.

'It's easy when you know what's at stake, Mira. In fact it's a very simple process, like a balancing act. Imagine that the path through life is a tightrope across the most beautiful valley. To get across you must learn to use a balancing pole. I teach you how to use the balancing pole but you will master the art only through continual practice. As you take each step your attention is always on keeping balance. As you get more adept you can take time to enjoy the view, to take in the sights and sounds around you, but there will be a part of you that will always have full attention placed on balancing. If you lose that attention even for one second then you will falter. If you become totally distracted then you will fall. It's that simple and that serious. Keep the consequences in mind, then placing the attention where it needs to be gets the priority it deserves.'

'Thank you Master,' Mira said quietly. 'Once again you remind me where my true focus must be.'

'Good,' he said briskly. 'Now let's take a rest. We have covered a lot today.'

Act XV

A moth flew into the room as she slept. It spread its wings. Dark shadows fell from its tips. It looked smug. It almost cackled to itself as it silently swirled and swooped. The shadows fell in circles behind it. The air grew cold.

Something woke her. She felt herself wake but she couldn't move. She sensed a presence in the room. She heard it shuffle along the floor and pull itself onto the bed. A small knobbled creature crawled towards her. Long cold fingers reached under her neck and under her knees. The creature reeked of malevolence. She was terrified. She had never experienced such terror. She kept trying to tell herself that she was dreaming but she couldn't make the dream stop. The window blew open and she felt the creature lift her from her body. The creature began to float, carrying her with it, towards the open window. Her heart pounded. Her mind went blank. The sense of horror was so pervasive that she forgot everything she had ever known. She had no sense that her partner must be there, sleeping next to her. All she could feel was darkness. A void of nothingness that was so absent that it threw up the most searing pain she had ever felt. All she knew was that if that creature got her to the open window she was lost.

She was drenched in a cold clammy sweat. The fear became even more overwhelming. The darkness was suffocating. She tried to calm herself.

'I have to get a grip,' she screamed at her self. 'I have to find a way to fight this.'

Somewhere, in a dim recess in her being, she heard a tiny whisper: *Even in your darkest hour you are not abandoned.* Her sense of dread was so all consuming that she couldn't really grasp what the whisper meant. Her mind felt like it was spinning out of control as wave upon wave of complete panic engulfed her. She tried to hear the whisper again. Something in the words had jogged her memory. As she grabbed desperately for the words, she suddenly thought of her master and of all he had taught her. She couldn't believe that in her terror she had forgotten he even existed.

As she remembered, another voice seemed to shout at her – 'HE'S RUBBISH. HE'S FILLED YOUR HEAD WITH RUBBISH. IT'S NOT REAL.'

She tried to shake her head but she was paralysed.

'That's not true,' she muttered to herself, over and over again. 'That's not true. The heart never lets go. My experience was real. The teaching was real, not just a theory. I WILL trust it. I WILL!'

She felt a rush of strength. An inner knowing dawned. The fear began to dissolve.

'YOU CAN TAKE MY BODY AWAY, BUT YOU CAN NEVER TAKE ME AWAY FROM THE FEELING I GET WITHIN. IT DOESN'T LEAVE ME. IT'S ALWAYS THERE!' she felt herself scream at the creature.

She focused on her heart with all her strength. She felt a wash of peace ripple through her body. The most beautiful music she had ever heard tinkled in every direction. She felt a perfect stillness settle in her heart. The creature stiffened. An almost potent sense of hatred and anger emanated from it. The creature raged, but she felt its powerlessness as it lost all control of her. She landed on the bed with a thump and opened her eyes.

She sat up in bed. Her heart was beating so hard that she could scarcely breathe. She was drenched with perspiration. Her partner mumbled 'whasamatter' sleepily. 'Oh God I just had the worst nightmare,' she whispered. 'I think I'm having a heart attack!' He cuddled her. 'S'ok. Go back to sleep now. I'm here, you're perfectly safe,' he muttered. She lay there afraid to close her eyes in case the nightmare would return. When she eventually drifted off, she slept fitfully.

The next morning she woke up and the dream was

rooted in her mind with the solidity of a memory. Something had changed in her though. She felt strangely elated. She tried to identify what it was. Then, like a flash, it dawned on her, she had lost her fear. She realised that deep down she had still held a fear of the unknown, of death, of evil or whatever you wanted to call it. She felt that she had been through a battle and had won. But how had she won? She thought about it. Then she saw that she had just been handed an understanding of the nature of darkness. She recognised that fear itself was the very thing the darkness fed on.

'Fear is the fuel and the engine,' she murmured. 'To exist it needed my undivided attention! It could overpower me only when my focus was so totally absorbed on the sense of fear that my own surrender to it was what gave it strength.'

She understood now that she had not become unafraid, rather, she had turned from fear and had trusted that love would protect her. It was a simple as that. She had changed the direction of her attention. She had reached out and love had responded and pulled her back.

'My God,' she muttered to herself, 'it's taken me this long to realise that this really works; this long to truly believe that the realm of the heart is a true reality!'

Act XVI

She was back on the pathway and had arrived at an old ruin. She looked at it blankly, not quite taking it in. She was preoccupied. Her brush with the nature of darkness had taken her to another level of understanding. She had lost her fear, but in doing so she felt strange. New sensations coursed through her that she hadn't yet managed to process fully. Most of all she felt very humbled and very, very small.

Her master arrived and looked at her quizzically. She burst into tears and told him all about her experience of the night before.

'So why the tears when you learned something so significant?' he asked.

'Because I'm so grateful,' she sobbed. 'I wouldn't understand any of this without you! Without you I'd be nothing at all. I am nothing without you.'

He stiffened. His eyes narrowed and she could feel the rage brewing in him.

'Nothing!' he shouted at her. 'NOTHING! Are you telling me that I've spent all my effort on a nothing? If this is how you value your existence then you have wasted my time. If all that I teach brings you to this conclusion then you really have learned nothing at all!'

He stormed off. She was stunned. She couldn't believe his reaction. Her legs felt like jelly. She wanted to run after him and beg for forgiveness but something told her that it would only make things worse. She slumped on the grass, feeling a rush of self pity.

'How appropriate that I'm sitting outside a ruin because I've just destroyed everything,' she thought.

She began to cry again. Then suddenly she stopped.

'I've lost my master,' she thought to herself, 'but I haven't lost the experience inside so I'll go there and figure out what to do.'

She closed her eyes and let the stillness settle. As she did so she became aware of the gentle beat of her heart and the rhythmic flow of her breath, entering and leaving her body. She saw the world fuse into one giant heartbeat floating on the supreme breath of existence. She flowed in and out of the world. She saw the vibrancy of life dancing on every atom of creation. Then she saw herself. She watched herself turn to look in a mirror and saw that the reflection in the mirror was a grotesque monster. She saw herself laugh as she put her hand right into the mirror to stir the now liquid glass.

'Dear little monster,' she heard herself say, 'I can't help but love and understand you too, even though sometimes you are such a meddlesome part of me.'

As the molten glass bubbled she watched the image of the monster melt into her reflected image.

'The resolution of duality,' she thought to herself with a sigh. 'That was no nightmare it was just me meeting an aspect of myself.'

She shook her head

'No wonder he was angry,' she thought sadly. 'I hadn't taken the time to really understand all I had experienced.'

She opened her eyes. He was sitting on a rock just across from her. He had a tight-lipped expression. She approached him cautiously.

'I'm truly sorry,' she said. 'I'm not nothing. I'm everything. The darkness lives in me too and in meeting it head on I was thrown. I am so appreciative of what you teach me, and I feel such love for you because of all you teach me, that I forgot that the very essence of what you teach is to value my own existence.'

He looked at her sternly.

'You did well. You came through the process of really understanding the nature of darkness but then you lost focus and, in the next breath, just let your mind gush without any thought to what you were saying. Forgetting, even for a moment, is sloppy consciousness, because, as you have just learned, the mind is capable of manifesting the most profound darkness. On this journey there is no room for lapses of consciousness. Every unconscious moment sets the seeds for a future disaster.'

She bit her lip and stared at the ground.

'Don't do that,' he said sharply. 'I don't want any martyrdom act. Hold your head up and look me in the eye when I speak to you.'

She raised her head and met his gaze head on.

'This is not about control or about pretending to feel something, just because you expect to or because you think I expect it. Understanding this experience has to be a real feeling. Now tell me what feeling you are having as we speak.'

'I'm feeling guilty that I made you angry,' she replied, 'and guilty and regretful also that I jumped to the conclusion that I had fully understood the nature of darkness before I really had understood it all.'

'Well at least that's honest, so we have a good starting point. The mind and the heart may occupy different realms but a clear heart can lend clarity and strength to the mind. The heart is never ignorant but the mind can be. The mind is a tool for you to use, in the same way as you would use a hand or a foot. You would not let your foot dictate your life to you would you?'

She laughed and shook her head.

'What is a foot?' he asked.

'It's a part of the body used for moving,' she replied.

'How does it do the moving?' he asked.

'It uses muscle and nerves and things like that,' she replied.

'Well, silly as it might seem, the mind is also just like a foot. It is like a big thinking muscle, powered by chemical information and nerves. It operates to keep all the life processes moving. It is not a function or a responsibility of the mind to seek fulfilment or peace. That would be alien to its inherent programme. Its function is to think; to come up with ideas, to dream, to imagine and to innovate. The mind is as it is. It is like a giant train that has to keep on going. It has to steam ahead. It will stop at a station only to shout out the name of the next station on the route. You can get on or off at any of the stations but sooner or later you will have to catch the next train.'

He paused and looked thoughtfully at the ruin.

'Ambition and desire fuel this train,' he continued. 'Once this deserted ruin was somebody's dream. Somebody took the trouble to build it, to furnish it, to make it look grand and imposing. Then time passed and better styles came along and this building, that had once meant so much to someone now means nothing. It's the same in life, we strive after something until we achieve it and almost instantaneously, as soon as the desire is attained, a bigger, better desire springs up to take its place. Boredom isn't accidental, it's the tool the mind uses to keep us moving on.'

'But what about experiencing and enjoying this life?' she asked. 'How is it that the mind allows that to happen because, after all, fulfilment is a calm state that exists beyond desire and ambition?'

'The mind doesn't allow it to happen at all,' he replied. 'If we were only our minds there would be no fulfilment. It would be abnormal for the mind to feel at peace; that is not its function. To even think about mind control is ridiculous. But, remember our discussion about quantum particles and the divine spark within. We are not just mind, we are also heart. Inner stillness comes from the heart not the mind. Fulfilment is about spending time in another place. The mind doesn't like that it can be escaped. It will try anything to pull you back to its total control even if that very grip becomes a darkness that can destroy you. That doesn't make the mind the enemy. It isn't. It just has no concept of the other you and, regardless, it likes to be in control. The mind can't inform the heart, but the heart can inform the mind. Thankfully we were given the tools to access the infinite self, the heart, the place that loves and appreciates the mind, but which is not bound or controlled by it.'

'So that is why fear can be so powerful,' she said thoughtfully. 'It's a way for the mind to take control if you're not aware of how it operates.'

He nodded.

'The mind is a vast storehouse of information. Nothing is discarded. Everything stays in there – the silly, the profound, the horrible, the pleasant. Clarity of feeling and the experience of consciousness are necessary in order to sift what the mind throws up. This is why the path of self-knowledge is long and requires dedication. The connection with the heart has to be maintained through regular practice. It is another language and, like any language, irregular use lessens the ability to communicate and understand.'

'That is why you were angry with me. You wanted me to realise the importance of clarity. I can see now that even the feelings of guilt and regret were just ways to allow myself to be distracted from real understanding. My heart was thankful and full of love but my head was telling me that I had failed and that I was a bad, stupid, worthless person who'd never get it right!'

'You got it in one!' he said with a grin. 'Feel before you speak, then what you say will really come from you. Then it will not be just an outburst of random thoughts backfiring.'

She smiled softly to herself as she turned back to the path. She felt that at last she was beginning to find a true clarity emerging in her own self and now she felt the need to take some time alone to process this.

Act XVII

The path led on from the ruin. She walked along drinking in the sights and sounds around her. Night was falling and she wanted to spend some time in silence. She came to the shores of a vast lake. The sky was now a rich midnight blue and the stars flickered in its depths. The clear waters of the lake formed a perfect mirror image of the scene above.

'As above so below,' she thought, smiling softly to herself.

She sat and turned within.

One breath in...
One breath out...

One breath in...
One breath out...

As she flowed with her breath she felt herself dissolve and merge with the infinite.

Her heart sparkled and shone. She was filled with a song that came from within her and from everywhere at once:

I am lost to the world

My heart is an ocean of tranquillity

Bliss is my sustenance

I am drunk on the abundance of your giving

Like rapturous lovers

we exchange breath after breath

I curl softly in the embrace of your heart

You take your bow of infinity

and pluck the chant of the universe

From the deepest stirrings of my soul

You curl softly in the embrace of my heart

Always there, waiting for me to find you

Filling me with sweet longing

Knowing that at your call

I will return

To drink once again

from the fountain of your giving

The music rained down on her, filling her being with bliss, pounding her heart with a kaleidoscope of colour, drenching her soul in the purest, coolest water. She opened her eyes and it seemed as though everything around her was joining in this song of life.

Act XVIII

Mira felt her heart flutter. As she slowly came back to herself, she gazed at the full moon overhead. It was so bright that she could see everything around her bathed in its silver hue.

She listened to the gentle swish of the water as it lapped softly against the shore. She couldn't resist the pull of the moonlight dancing on the surface of the lake so she decided to go for a swim.

The water lapped with a hypnotic beat

…Lub-dup…Lub-dup…

'Is that my heart thumping, or my soul?' she idly wondered to herself as she floated in the soothing waters. She was embraced in a circle of sound and the moonlight seemed to ebb and flow in time with her every movement. She saw the threads of her existence span out. They glowed and shone in the silvery light to become a tapestry of experience. Lifetime after lifetime, she saw the dance of her own journey unfold. Each life had brought her a step closer to fulfilment. Yet she saw that whether or not such lives had even taken place was irrelevant. They were past selves, now gone. Only this moment was real. Knowing who she may have been didn't matter. Now she was Mira and she would never be Mira again. This lifetime was the experience she had to seize, and in this lifetime she had everything. Just as she had learned to trust that what was to come would be taken care of, she had to trust that whatever had gone before, whatever learning and experience was meant for her, had been incorporated into the person that was now Mira.

As she moved slowly through the water she thought of all the people in her life. Her heart felt full of love. She thought of each person and the ways in which just knowing them enriched her life. She laughed to herself, thinking that even the bad times, the fights, the arguments, the angry silences had helped her to learn more about her own self. She hoped that in turn she was contributing to their lives and resolved to be even more appreciative of every moment spent with each of them.

She swam back to the shore. As she was drying herself, she noticed a little oratory tucked amongst the trees. She went to explore. The door was open and the church glowed with candlelight. The décor was spartan, just simple stone walls and plain wooden benches facing a large window overlooking the lake. The moon was framed in the window drawing the quiet peace of the scene outside into the simple serenity of the building. Sitting quietly on one of the benches was a young nun. She looked up at Mira and smiled.

'It's beautiful isn't it,' she remarked, glancing appreciatively at the moon.

Mira returned her smile and nodded in agreement.

'I just took a swim, I couldn't resist. It was so warm and the moon is so huge tonight that I felt like it was calling me!' Mira remarked with a laugh.

'The return to the waters,' the nun said quietly.

'Like a giant moon-womb,' Mira murmured.

'Don't you think it's amazing that we begin our human life in water and in darkness? And isn't it interesting that water and darkness are often the very things we develop phobias about as we grow up?' the nun commented.

Mira sat beside her.

'I'm learning that it's all about trust, trust and unlearning,' Mira said. 'We learn not to trust and we learn to be afraid. While an element of both may be necessary in day to day life, when it comes to fulfilment we have to find that starting point of trust all over again.'

The nun smiled.

'And acceptance,' she added, as she turned to face Mira. 'We have to accept that the full picture isn't always revealed. Like with the moon, it only ever shows us one face. The other side is always turned away, we never see it with our own eyes but we know it's there.'

'You've devoted your life to the other side haven't you, the life we can only feel?' Mira questioned.

'I've devoted my life to a particular way of life,' the nun replied. 'But from what you say you seem to be as moved by the inner life as I am.'

Mira laughed.

'Perhaps. But I'm certainly not cut out for abstinence, chastity and poverty – that is if they are the vows that you have to take!' Mira exclaimed.

'It's horses for courses,' the nun replied with a soft laugh. 'I don't think that what path is actually chosen matters, it's how it's lived that's important. If the only way to be fulfiled was my way then it would be a world of all or nothing wouldn't it? Everyone outside the religious life would be dead to the experience within and that would truly be a sad state. As it stands many who profess to follow a religion can be ignorant of the experience within and many who say they have no time at all for religion are very aware of the experience within.'

'Well I don't have a religion because I feel that the divine is everywhere and not just in one belief system or another,' Mira explained, 'but I don't mean by that that I'm against religions. I quite like bits of many of them. My Master says though, that the danger with a belief system is that the system can become more important than the experience, then wars can break out.'

'That's very true unfortunately,' the nun replied. 'Most religions began with a Master. When the Master passes on, then the religions spring up with all the interpretations and arguments that follow. My little way is to try to see the face of God in all that I do and to stay as close as possible to what my Master originally taught.'

'What did your Master teach?' Mira asked.

'That the kingdom of Heaven is within', the nun replied.

'That is what my Master teaches also', Mira replied. 'Don't you think it's strange that all the Master's seem to teach the same thing. It makes you wonder why there ever has to be more than one Master, doesn't it?'

The nun smiled.

'As long as the heart is beating, the need for the Master exists', she said. 'It is the truth of the message that is important. I believe that God will do whatever it takes and send as many kinds of messengers as are necessary to get his message of love to as many hearts as possible. Everyone has different needs. Some like to have a living Master in the here and now with whom they can interact externally and internally. Then there are those like me who are content to have an internal connection only. It is the connection that is important.

All the rest, the structures, the rituals, the practices are just add-ons. They are the bits that some enjoy and for which others have no need.'

'But you like the structure of religious life,' Mira said.

'I do', the nun replied. ' I find the structure of religious life helpful to me for my own self-discipline. When my heart falters, which it often does, I can lean on the structures. And when my heart is singing, the structures melt into the song. What do you do when your heart falters Mira?'

Mira paused and gave the question some consideration.

'I see what you're saying', she replied thoughtfully, 'and though I don't have a religious structure, I do have to remember to spend time within myself every day, even though there are days that I don't want to. I suppose there can never be a path without a structure of some kind. There has to be a place you can lean on in the bad times. You can strip almost everything away on my chosen path, except the necessity of spending time within. It's only when I'm quiet inside that I can really hear what I am being taught.'

'So though we might seem poles apart, we're not so different really', the nun said gently.

'It seems not, who would ever have thought it!' Mira replied with a soft giggle.

They chatted for a while, sharing stories of their experiences and their lives. Then, as it was getting late, they had to end their conversation.

'I'm glad to have met you here,' the nun said warmly to Mira. 'My life is sheltered and I'm not always aware that people in the world are striving for more. All I hear are the bad news stories.'

'Well I'll make a pact with you,' Mira said brightly. 'I'll come back to see you with positive reports and you remember me in your prayers, and that way I'll feel like I've an insurance policy!'

They hugged each other warmly, then continued on their separate ways.

Act XIX

Dawn was breaking and the sun began to pour across the sky. A shimmering butterfly seemed to dance in the rays of the sun. The butterfly flapped its wings. It became the sunlight and flowed down on Mira, gently caressing the crown of her head. She closed her eyes, relishing the feeling and when she opened them again he was there.

'How are you?' he asked.

'Blissful,' she replied. 'Last night I was so filled with joy I thought I'd burst, and today I feel even more pouring in! It's like there's no limit to this feeling.'

'There isn't!' he said with a chuckle. 'That's the magic of the inner cup. It grows with you. The more you experience, the more it can contain.'

She told him about her experiences of the night before and her talk with the nun.

He listened and nodded thoughtfully.

'Yes,' he said, 'when hearts are at peace there is no duality. The same sun shines on everyone. People may view it differently, they may choose to label it, interpret its activities, analyse its composition, but when it shines, everyone feels the same feeling of warmth.'

'I was thinking about something like that last night,'

she remarked. 'It feels at times that nature is like a big treasure hunt and, through what I'm experiencing, I keep finding that all the clues add up to finding the presence of the divine in all that I see and feel. Then I think of all the war and death and needless destruction and it upsets me. How can it ever be stopped? How can the world ever become a peaceful place?'

He laughed.

'The world!' he exclaimed. 'The world is a very peaceful rock floating in a very calm solar system. I don't see Earth rushing at Venus or Mars, challenging them to a fight! And it has a very fortunate position, if it was anywhere else, Earth could be constantly bombarded by meteors. Instead it's lucky to bump into something only every few million years or so. This world, this planet Earth, doesn't need to seek peace, it already has it. It is people who create the wars, the random acts of violence, the hatred and destruction. And yet inside every human being is the most perfect peace. Every individual heart must seek that peace, must become conscious that everything connects, that taking responsibility for making the world a better place starts first within each person. Unconscious behaviour has a heavy cost.'

'The heaviest cost being death,' she said.

'No,' he shook his head. 'The heaviest cost is in

failing to notice life.'

He looked at the sun and smiled at her.

'Nature is so beautifully set up to remind us,' he said softly. 'Like the sun, the divine is always there, even when we are not aware. Yet, on the darkest night, the sun still shines. It has to, because it is the source, the energy that powers this solar system and keeps it moving and changing. And, in case we forget, we have the moon.'

He laughed.

'You know the moon could have been made of anything, but it wasn't. We're very fortunate that the moon is composed of such a light coloured substance. Because of its pale colour it reflects the sun, so even when one half of the world is in darkness we can look up and see the light of the moon and know that the sun is still there.'

'A little beacon dancing up there in the sky,' she said dreamily.

'The difference between the sun and the divine,' he continued, 'is that you don't have a mini sun glowing inside you, but you do have a spark of the divine within, shining light of another sort.'

'And what about the moon?' she asked.

'The master is like the moon,' he replied. 'The master doesn't generate the power but the master can reflect it. The master lights the dark night of the soul to remind those who want to be reminded that everything we could ever wish for is contained within.'

'You make it real,' she said, 'for me anyway. I can see the sun and feel it, but I can only feel the divine. I don't think that I'd have arrived at that feeling in such a simple way if you hadn't shown me how.'

'Well you get out what you put in,' he commented. 'You can listen to everything I say, but if you never put time and effort into feeling it within your own self, then all my words are meaningless. Your own effort is necessary to keep it a living experience for you.'

'What would happen if I just kept turning within but stopped listening to what you teach?' she asked.

'Oh, I think you're head would fall off!' he chortled. 'Ha! Ha! That would make it easy for me wouldn't it! A captive audience – the only problem is that then we'd have two very undesirable elements, fear and compulsion. That wouldn't be a very good recipe for growth would it now?'

Laughing happily, she shook her head.

'Well,' he went on, 'the best way to look at me is to think of me as being like a plumber. There you are, you come with all your fittings built in and I just come along and connect you to the main water supply. Essentially that's it, my job is technically done, but to be a really good plumber I undertake to stay in contact so that when residue builds up I come along and clean the connection.'

She clapped her hands.

'That's great!' she exclaimed. 'My very own plumber!'

'Mmm..' he smiled. 'You see the world is full of distractions and it always creates new distractions that can build up and lead you to become unclear. The master will remind you over and over to pay attention to that which will keep you clear. The master will do what is necessary to keep that connection flowing. And the master won't always be polite about it. Sometimes the master will shout and make things seem very unpleasant if that is what it takes. The one constant though is love and when the student feels that love and is receptive to it, then confusion melts away and the beauty of the heart unfolds.'

'It really is a dance isn't it?' she said. 'The master, the student and the experience within, all flowing together.'

'Yes it is,' he replied. 'When all three are in step then the divine is manifest. When the divine is felt then there is no need for analysis, speculation, or doubt. Who doubts that the breath exists and yet who has seen the source of breath?'

The path ahead became wider. As they walked on together, she could see the garden in the distance. She was almost back at where she had started.

Act XX

She had a dream that she was dreaming. In each dream she turned to watch her dreaming self. Each self in turn asked aloud, 'who is the dreamer and who is dreamed?' In between each self a golden butterfly fluttered. Its wings were tipped with a deep rich pink, its little face shone a pure white.

She heard a voice somewhere in the distance.

'Wake up Mira,' it called, over and over again.

She opened her eyes and saw him standing over her. He was smiling, his eyes sparkling with mirth.

'You were out cold!' he said. 'I've been calling you for a while.'

She looked around. She was back in the garden, stretched out comfortably in a deck chair. She saw the crystal door shimmering in the distance. She rubbed her eyes sleepily.

'Oh, I was so deeply asleep, and I was having the strangest dream,' she mumbled. 'It was a dream about dreaming and I felt that same peculiar feeling that you get when you're half awake and half asleep – you know what I mean, when in that split second between sleeping and waking it's hard to know what's real and what's a dream.'

'The world lies somewhere in between,' he said softly, as he sat in the chair next to hers.

She leaned forward and pulled her chair into an upright position.

'Am I the dreamer or the dreamed?' she asked mischievously.

He cast a sideways glance at her.

'Perhaps you need to look elsewhere. If the dreamer and the dreamed can both be seen then who is asking the question?'

She paused, then smiled slowly, nodding as she did so.

'My conscious self. When I'm unaware then I may as well be unconscious, asleep to the world around me. When I'm trying to rationalise it and figure it out using the judgements and measurements I apply to day to day life, then I may as well be asleep because the rules of the finite can never really know how the world of the infinite operates.'

'That's correct, but it can be expressed with more simplicity. If the master could utter only one word to the student it would simply be 'Awaken!'. To go through life unaware of the world inside is to live as if asleep. All the time is spent in repetition of activity, patterns of behaviour, needs, wants, desires and ambitions. Like a giant loop tape, life lived in that way just becomes an endlessly repeating circle. It becomes a treadmill, miles are covered but the feet never leave the same spot, no progress is achieved.'

'But living has value,' she argued. 'People interacting with each other with love, creating great music and art, having the ambition to make the most of life...'

'Living consciously has value,' he replied, 'because living consciously leads to an appreciation of every moment given. To awaken does not negate the experience of day to day life. It just reminds that the time here is limited. Life is a precious gift, but not every-one opens the package. Not appreciating life doesn't always mean that bad things happen, sometimes it means just letting life slip by.'

He sat back and looked at the garden. A pair of crimson butterflies darted to and from a bed of deep yellow roses.

'Who would think they had once been caterpillars,' he remarked, indicating to the butterflies.

'Perhaps there's some butterfly who goes around to all the caterpillars and tries to get them to believe that one day they will be just the same,' she giggled.

'There's a story about that very thing!' he said with a wry grin. 'As I get the feeling that you don't want to go back through that door just yet, I'll tell you.'

He settled back in the chair and began.

"Once there was a brother caterpillar and a sister caterpillar. The sister spent all her time looking to the sky. She would watch the birds and all the other winged creatures with longing. She said to her brother 'One day I'll fly just like them. I really feel that I will.'

Her brother was scornful.

'Don't be so stupid,' he said. 'What would you even want to fly for. It's lovely to be able to wiggle along the earth and to find a fat juicy leaf. I watch those silly birds and they're always just darting about looking useless.'

She listened to him, but didn't agree.

'It's not that I don't like being a caterpillar and that I don't enjoy every leaf and patch of earth that we explore, but I just can't shake off the feeling that there's something more. Haven't you ever wondered why there are no old caterpillars? Where does everyone go?'

Her brother looked angry.

'You are so STUPID,' he shouted. 'Why do you think those birds are so fat? That's where we all end up – in their stomachs. We're bird food! We just have a pointless reason here. It's as simple as that. There's nothing ahead except some sharp beak, then darkness. Just accept that and stop going on at me. And stop admiring the very creatures you should hate!'

Her brother was disgusted and wriggled away.

She curled on her little leaf singing happily to herself.

'Maybe my brother is right, but it's still lovely to look at all the other creatures,' she said to herself.

Just then a dragonfly whirred past. He saw her on the leaf and landed to say 'hello'.

She told him about her argument with her brother. The dragonfly clicked and hummed with laughter.

'But of course you'll fly. One day you'll be a butterfly!'

She was thrilled and excitedly went to tell her brother.

'And you believed him!' he scoffed. 'No one believes that mad fool. Even the very word, "butterfly", I've never heard anything so ridiculous.'

Time passed and the urge came for the caterpillars to start spinning their chrysalises. She was full of hope, sure that this was going to take her towards her dream. Her brother was melancholy.

'This is just packing you know,' he said sadly. 'It's a cruel trick. They've engineered it that we do this to fill their stomachs even more. We're too thin as we are.'

She tried to argue with him but he wouldn't listen.

They hung, suspended in their chrysalises, for what seemed like an eternity. Then one day her chrysalis began to move. She felt it slip away. She couldn't figure out where she was, everything looked red. She shook herself and a trickle of red fluid gathered at her little feet. As she looked down she noticed the most beautiful sight. She had wings of lilac and gold with little green spots for decoration. She flapped her wings and began to fly. It was the most amazing feeling. She landed on a flower and sipped delicately at the nectar. It was exquisite, beyond any taste she could have ever imagined. As she looked down on the earth below she felt extraordinarily privileged.

'This is even better than being a bird,' she sang out loud, 'because they have only ever been birds. But I know how cosy and warm it is to snuggle in the warm earth and to chew the deep green leaves and now I know the joy of flight and the magical taste of nectar. I have been given two lives, two experiences in this one lifetime.'

She heard a grumbling coming from a rich yellow flower. Perched on the flower was a beautiful orange butterfly. It was her brother! She flew excitedly to him.

'It wasn't a trick, it was real,' she cried, fluttering her wings to him in greeting.

He looked bitter.

'Don't be so naive!' he snapped. 'Look at the colour of us both. You bright gold and me bright orange.

They'll see us for miles. We won't last a second I tell you!'

'Oh brother! Why can't you see how amazing this is? You're beautiful. And we can fly!'

He grimaced.

'What sort of awful stuff is this?' he moaned, indicating to the nectar. 'My teeth are gone. I can't get a bite of leaf no matter how I try. And I hate flying. It makes my head spin. I tried to curl nicely on a leaf but these blasted wings keep slipping so I fall down.'

She shook her little head and spiralled upwards, realising that there was nothing that she could do to change his mind. He was as determined to dislike their new life as she was to embrace it.

'Perhaps in time he will like it more,' she thought, as she caught a current of air and swooped and fluttered along it into the blue, blue sky."

He raised his eyebrows as he looked at her.

'You win some, you lose some,' he remarked light-heartedly.

'The gift of choice,' she said.

He nodded.

'And the harsh reality that judgement can create,' he added. 'To become so fixed in concepts that the concept rules and the reality of experience is negated.'

Mira was pensive.

'Life is a tour of hearts' he murmured, 'like with this garden, each person will respond to it differently. Some will see the beauty and the balance. Some will see only the thorns, the weeds and the mud. The garden is constantly evolving. The gardener is always there shaping it, tending it, trying new ideas and styles. Some will walk though this garden, enjoy it for a while then will trip over and fall. Instead of just getting back up again, they will say the garden is now ruined for them. They will blame the gardener for not keeping the garden all the same level. They will blame nature for being so chaotic and will resolve never to set foot in the garden again. But they will never admit that perhaps they should have been watching where they put their feet!'

She giggled softly.

'It may sound funny, but sadly that is how many people live. There are people,' he added, 'like the little brother caterpillar who want it to be just like they imagine it should be and so can never accept or enjoy it for what it really is. They waste lifetimes obsessing about what they would prefer it to be and what they would do with it if it were in their control.'

'But there is no control,' she said thoughtfully. 'The journey is the destination. That is something that I understand more and more every day. Life has become a very magical experience.'

They sat for a time, quietly enjoying the beauty and the peace of the garden. Then he got up and began to walk towards the door. She followed him slowly. She knew she had to return, but a part of her wanted to stay and listen to him forever.

Act XXI

He gestured to the doorway.

'Well there it is. Now it's time for you to go back and to apply all you have learned in your own life. Are you ready to continue your journey through life?'

She nodded, glancing cautiously at the doorway. The crystal supports shone in the morning sun.

He looked at her thoughtfully.

'The true miracle of life lies in the breath and in the ability to experience the divine within. There are no other miracles,' he added, 'plenty of unusual phenomena maybe, but no other miracles. Too often the unusual takes over and the truly miraculous is forgotten.'

She took a deep breath and turned to him. Silence fell, and she could feel her emotions well up.

'How can I ever thank you?' she asked, as the tears fell down her cheeks. 'The gift of your teaching is something I can never repay. Before I had this experience I was fine. I didn't think there was anything missing. But through experiencing the feeling within, life is so much richer. I can only promise you that I will continue to listen and to learn.'

He smiled.

'Remember above all that life is fun', he said. 'There is no limit to the depth of experience within, and there is no limit to the amount of experiences life will throw at you. Good times will come and go. Bad times will come and go. That is the nature of life. There is no way to avoid it. Let your experience of what is within be your shelter. It is the calm place. The storms may blow all around, but they can never reach within. To be able to learn, even from adversity, is both a gift to be treasured and a skill to be practised. It is not always easy and it is not always hard, but it is always simple. However complicated a situation may appear, when it is approached with a heart full of love and clarity, then a simple solution always emerges because the rule of the heart is simple. It asks only 'Am I fulfiled?' If the answer is yes, then go with it. If it's no, then get away from whatever it is as fast as you can. The mind will throw up all the *ifs* and *buts* and *shoulds* and *coulds*. The heart will cast them aside and bring you back to that simple question. The mind is a tool to be used with wisdom and clarity. Question everything until you are sure that what you feel is informed by the true language of the heart and not a concept created by the mind.'

'I understand that there will always be ups and downs,' she said, wiping her tears away, 'but you have taught me how to feel my way through life. Taking the time to be still each day not only fills me with joy, it also gives me a perspective that allows me to at least attempt to weed out faulty concepts as they emerge.'

'To keep trying is the most important part. What did I tell you about mistakes?' he asked.

'To pick myself up, dust myself down, take responsibility for my part, then move on. No looking back,' she replied.

'Good, remember that,' he said gently.

She nodded.

'It is a magical journey,' he said. 'As you continue on, never forget that I am right behind you, every step of the way. But my teaching has value only when you return regularly to your experience inside. It is your balancing pole and your safety net all rolled into one. Stay vigilant and let no room for doubt in your heart. Every task you take on in life, undertake to do it well and do it joyfully. Treat everyone with respect, but shun all those who would have you embrace the darkness. The only constant is trust. Trust the process and every step you take will lead you to the doors of ever-deeper experience.

Be conscious and above all else be fulfiled. Like the sunflower keep your face turned to the divine and the blessings will pour down to warm and nourish your heart.'

His eyes danced with love and his smile radiated to her heart. She smiled back at him, then turned to walk through the door.

A white butterfly flitted and danced in the breeze. It flew to her as if in recognition. Then it darted ahead, looping and spiralling in the warm breeze, before fluttering down to the snowy-softness of the heather beds. At the first sip of nectar, its wings stilled, its little body now fully focused on the business of fulfilment.

Mira sent a silent farewell to the busy butterfly and continued on. She felt a rush of excitement. She didn't close the door behind her. There was no need. From now on the world within her heart would be open to flow through the journey that was her life.

* * *

When I turn within and start to understand
the preciousness of this existence, then I can dance.
And the dance is so simple.
It is the most private of dances. Nobody watches.
This dance is real. This dance is for me. It is my expression
and my gratitude — feeling thankful for this life.
(Maharaji)

In short, there are three things that last:
faith, hope and love;
and the greatest of these is love.
(1 Corinthians 13:13)

Quotations

Act IX

Line quoted from *Solitude Standing,* a song by Suzanne Vega
from the album of the same name, A & M Records 1987
Lines quoted from 'The Second Coming' by WB Yeats

Act X I

Information on parietal lobe activity inspired by an article
entitled 'The Science of God' by Vince Rause (Reader's
Digest March 2002)

I apologise now for anything I might have missed and will
correct anything brought to my attention in subsequent
editions.

Cover Painting

'Frau in der Morgensonne' painted by Casper David Freidrich
in 1818, reproduced courtesy of Museum Folkwang, Essen

Acknowledgments

This book is a reflection of my learning and my interpretation of what I have been taught and does not claim to speak on anyone's behalf in any way. Likewise the character of the master in this book, though loosely based on my actual teacher, is a fictionalised portrait and should not be taken to be a direct representation of an actual person, people or events.

Thanks to my friends and family who had to endure me constantly banging on about 'the book' and for reading and offering suggestions throughout the draft stages. In particular my parents - John & Kathy, also Fred, Mary, Rosie, Donal, Heather, Varsha, Casey, Carol, Margaret, Eileen, Maggie, Gillian, Cecelia, Dee and Ja.

Special thanks to...

My 'heart' teacher, Prem Rawat Maharaji - www.tprf.org - for his wisdom, his laughter and his neverending patience and perseverance. In teaching me the language of the heart he made the teachings and the lives of all the great masters (and life itself!) come to life for me.

Bessie O'Flynn for teaching me how to write and Sr Angela for opening my mind to the wonders of the universe through her appreciation both of God and of Physics!

The Butterfly

The butterfly has long been seen as a symbol of the soul and of transformation.

From the earthbound caterpillar to the free flying, but fragile, butterfly, we can see in this insect the possibility, and the actuality, of transformation. In turn we see the need to protect a creature so delicate that its wings can be torn apart by driving rain.

In addition, according to Chaos Theory a seemingly insignificant event can cause dramatic consequences. It is this interpretation that most inspired the symbolism of the butterfly in this book. Chance meetings and small learnings can transform a life, so the image of the butterfly was used in this book to herald the little steps along the way that, when taken together, are the keys to the discovery and the liberation of the inner self.

www.katy-press.com

katypress@eircom.net

This book can be ordered direct from Katy Press
or from www.amazon.co.uk

Contact information:
Katy Press, 2 Barrack Street, Bantry, Co Cork, Ireland.